"Do you like children, Josie?"

Luke had no idea what this conversation was doing to her, and she drew on every scrap of strength she had won over the last few years. "I suppose so. I don't really come into contact with any," she said.

"The original career woman?"

Josie felt he disapproved of her, and it hurt. "You don't get to the top by playing happy families," she said levelly.

"No, I guess you don't. But you sure as hell miss a lot if you don't." Luke stared at her, hard.

He thought she was an ambitious career woman, hell-bent on getting to the very top? Well, it was an impression she had deliberately fostered....

FROM HERE TO PATERNITY—romances that feature fantastic men who *eventually* make fabulous fathers. Some seek paternity, some have it thrust upon them. All will make it—whether they like it or not!

HELEN BROOKS lives in Northamptonshire, England, and is married with three children. As she is a committed Christian, busy housewife and mother, her spare time is at a premium but her hobbies include reading and walking her two energetic and very endearing young dogs. Her long-cherished aspiration to write became a reality when she put pen to paper on reaching the age of forty, and sent the result off to Harlequin.

Look out for *Husband By Contract* and *Second Marriage* by Helen Brooks, coming soon. Two romances linked by a deeply emotional theme...

Husbands & Wives

Sometimes the perfect marriage is worth waiting for!

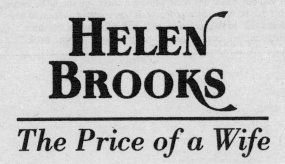

HELEN BROOKS

The Price of a Wife

Harlequin Books

TORONTO • NEW YORK • LONDON
AMSTERDAM • PARIS • SYDNEY • HAMBURG
STOCKHOLM • ATHENS • TOKYO • MILAN
MADRID • WARSAW • BUDAPEST • AUCKLAND

ISBN 0-373-11914-3

THE PRICE OF A WIFE

First North American Publication 1997.

Copyright © 1997 by Helen Brooks.

This edition published by arrangement with Harlequin Books S.A.

® and TM are trademarks of the publisher. Trademarks indicated with ® are registered in the United States Patent and Trademark Office, the Canadian Trade Marks Office and in other countries.

Printed in U.S.A.

CHAPTER ONE

'Josie? There's a man over there who's been staring at you for a good ten minutes. Do you know him?'

'Where?' As Josie turned, her wide, green-flecked eyes following Penny's glance across the crowded, noisy room, her face wasn't even faintly interested. She was used to men staring at her; it came with the territory. As one of the highest paid and most successful promotions executives in London, she knew she presented something of an anomaly to the average male—and one that wasn't always welcome in the male-dominated environment in which she worked.

Fine-boned and tiny, at five feet one, and with a mass of gleaming Titian-coloured hair, creamy skin and large expressive eyes in a golden honey shade liberally flecked with green, she wasn't exactly what they'd expected to see if her reputation had gone before her . . . and it invariably had.

Over the last ten years, since she had first entered the promotions rat race as a nervous but ambitious eighteen-year-old fresh from college, she had established herself as an astute and level-headed businesswoman with a flair for knowing exactly what appealed to the public. Her job was her life; she gave it one hundred per cent commitment and the rewards had been enormous.

'Hang on a minute,' Penny muttered impatiently to herself as the crowd surged and moved, the buzz of conversation fierce and loud. '*Now*. Look over there, next to the group from Chantals. He's still looking this way and you can't miss him.'

'Which . . . ?' Josie's voice trailed away as she met the full force of a pair of very intent, narrowed eyes set in a hard, tanned face that was all male and quite expressionless. The man was big, very big, darkly imposing and terribly out of place in this crowd of affected, pretentious sycophants who had arrived by invitation for the grand opening of Josie's

5

latest work project: a flamboyant, madly expensive art gallery in a city already full of art galleries. That much at least registered before she turned sharply away, her stomach lurching.

'Well? Do you know him?' Penny asked curiously, her mild brown eyes alight with interest. 'I know *I* don't. If I'd met a hunk like him before I wouldn't have forgotten.'

'No, no, I don't know him.' Josie's voice was cool and noncommittal, and not at all as she was feeling inside. She couldn't remember the last time a man's glance had affected her like this. She felt ridiculously disturbed and flustered—threatened, almost? She shook the thought away abruptly, furious with herself for allowing it to enter her mind in the first place.

Nerves. This was all just nerves, she told herself firmly. The same 'first night' agitation she suffered with all her projects until she knew she had got it right. There was no need to let her imagination run riot, useful though that particular attribute was in her line of work.

She drew herself up to her full five feet one and smiled at her assistant, who was a good six inches taller than herself. 'We need to circulate, Penny, admire a few pretty feathers and give the old sweet talk. I'll see you by the main door when the champagne and strawberries are served at seven, OK? We'll have done our duty by then and things will be winding down.'

'Fine.' Penny nodded obediently, her good-natured face setting in a practised smile as she plunged into the mêlée.

'Josie?' The owner of the art gallery, a successful and wealthy entrepreneur, who had his finger in more pies than Jack Horner, touched her softly on the arm as she turned. 'Brilliant success, girl—well done.' He nodded cynically at the richly dressed, somewhat theatrical assembly. 'Not exactly my type, if I'm being honest, but you sure pulled in all those who needed to be seen here for the gallery to have credibility.'

'That is what you paid me to do, Mr White.' She smiled carefully, her voice and face pleasant but reserved.

The small balding man in front of her had made it plain on more than one occasion that he wanted more than just her business expertise, but she was used to dealing with the Mr Whites of this world, and there was a surplus of them in the city. She was polite, courteous and very adept at deflecting even the most obvious come-on, but underneath the graciousness there was hard-won composure and a firm control that settled even the most ardent suitor when it became necessary. Like now.

'Quite so, my dear, quite so.' He patted her arm again, his round face already shiny with perspiration. 'How about a little drink to celebrate all your hard work when this lot have gone? I've got a suite for the weekend in—'

'I don't think so.' She moved an inch or so away, her expression still smiling but her meaning clear. 'I've got a good deal of preparation to do tonight for a meeting tomorrow morning.'

'You work too hard.' His tongue flicked reptilean-like over his lower lip, and she just managed to repress a shudder. 'You ought to have the weekends free to enjoy yourself.'

'I don't work every weekend, Mr White,' she said coolly, 'just when it's necessary. Now, if you'll excuse me, it looks as if Mr Puzo is at a loose end and needs company...' She turned and walked purposefully over to an influential art-dealer, engaging him in conversation until Mr White had drifted away.

At exactly seven o'clock she started to make her way to the door, but stopped abruptly when a sudden break in the crowd showed her who Penny was talking to. That man again. She stared at him, her eyes taking in every little detail of his appearance while she could view him unobserved as he concentrated on Penny.

She had felt his eyes on her more than once as she had circulated the room, had been vitally aware of his dark presence as he had stood somewhat aloof from the rest of the throng by one of the deep, recessed windows. But she had been careful not to let her glance meet his. Why, she didn't quite know.

Who was he? Her smooth brow wrinkled with curiosity. The guest list had been both exclusive and fashionable, and she had made it her business to be aware of the history of each personage represented there. However, most of the

names had had 'and partner' written next to them, so she
had no means of knowing either who he was with or anything about him other than what she could see. And she
had to admit what she could see was... disturbing.

There was a formidable authority about him, a hard,
masculine aura that sat on the big body almost challeng-
ingly. His hair was black, jet-black, and cut very short, as
though he had no time to waste on any sort of excessive
grooming, and he was expensively dressed. There was a
smooth designer cut to the dark grey suit he was wearing
that stood out like a sore thumb against the gaudy wild
clothes the art world indulged in.

He looked... She bit her lip, suddenly annoyed with
herself as the simile flashed into her mind. But he *did*. He
looked like a dangerous black panther amid a host of vain,
preening cockatoos, and the 'and partner' label sat badly
on such a man. She couldn't imagine him ever being an
appendage to anybody, but who, *who* was he with? And
who was *he*? And what was the colour of his eyes? *His
eyes*?

She flushed as hotly as if she had voiced the question
out loud. Why on earth did she care about the colour of
his eyes anyway? She had made up her mind years ago about
the road down which she would travel, *had* to travel, and
her plans didn't include any sort of romantic involvement—light or otherwise. She was being ridiculous,
crazy. Perhaps Mr White was right; perhaps she had been
working too hard lately. She'd certainly never had this
trouble with her imagination before.

'Josie, darling... Wonderful little reception, you clever
girl, you...'

She turned very slowly as she forced a social smile to her
face, recognising the voice of one of the female executives
from a rival firm. She didn't dislike Charlotte
Montgomery—in fact they shared the same sense of
humour, which had smoothed more than one difficult situation in the past—but she knew the other woman had been
working hard to secure this particular project, and magnanimity was not one of Charlotte's virtues.

'You have obviously got the right touch with Mr White; you'll have to let me in on your secret some time...' The words were lazy and without real malice, although their meaning was clear.

Josie knew Charlotte meant nothing personal—she just had to have a little twist of the knife to state her annoyance at losing out to the other woman—but this time Josie didn't like the innuendo. She had had enough sly digs along the same lines from male colleagues in the past, when her work had been superior to theirs, and she had expected more from Charlotte. Both of them were in highly paid jobs, doing good work and surviving on their own initiative and flair despite high odds, and she had thought—naïvely, perhaps, she acknowledged now—that Charlotte would respect that and leave the sexist talk to the men.

Well, she was blowed if she was going to defend herself. In fact...

'Well, you know how it is, Charlotte.' She gave the other woman a brilliant smile as she spoke. 'The old casting couch still has its uses.'

Charlotte acknowledged the game, set and match with a slight curve of her thin red mouth, but then her light blue eyes widened considerably at something just over Josie's left shoulder.

'Miss Owens?' The male voice was very deep, with a slight husky edge that was undeniably attractive. 'Your assistant tells me you are due to leave soon.'

She turned to face him slowly, knowing who it was even before her gaze moved up and up to meet the hard-boned face. Silver-grey. His eyes were silver-grey, she thought irrelevantly, like ice-cold honed steel.

'I...' He must have heard that last remark, she thought helplessly. How could she explain it had been a play on words, that Charlotte had known it was the very opposite to how it had sounded? 'I...' And then she took a firm grip on herself, years of training coming to her aid. 'I don't think we've met,' she said formally as she held out her hand politely. 'I'm Josie Owens.'

'Yes, I know.' He smiled coolly but it didn't reach the mesmerising eyes. 'Luke Hawkton. How do you do?'

His grip was firm and hard and strong, very much like the man himself, she surmised as she found her small hand engulfed in his, only to be released almost immediately.

Hawkton? Luke Hawkton? She had heard that name somewhere before, but for the moment the connection escaped her. It had clearly been just the name she had heard; if she had seen a picture of this man she would have remembered. It was an arresting face, not handsome or even good-looking in the normal run of things, but the cruel sensual mouth and hard, determined jawline spoke of dominant strength, as did the high cheekbones and cold, black-lashed eyes, and there was something about the whole that was far more magnetic than any stock attractiveness.

His dark aura was a subtle emanation of restrained power and authority, but there was something else, a sensual undertone, that brought tiny little flickers shivering down her spine. He was all male, utterly sure of himself, and she had no doubt that he could be as ruthless as the lithe, hard-planed panther she had mentally compared him to earlier. A man to be avoided at all costs, in fact.

'Miss Owens?' She suddenly became aware that she had been staring at him almost vacantly for a good fifteen seconds, and that the faintly slanted silver-grey eyes held a thread of amusement in their cool depths. 'I asked if I could have a word with you,' he prodded smoothly.

'Of course.' Charlotte hadn't moved from the spot, and now Josie turned to include the tall blonde as she spoke. 'This is Charlotte Montgomery, a colleague of mine,' she said with a wave of her hand, but the silver eyes barely brushed Charlotte's face. He gave her a polite nod and then took Josie's arm in his hand and guided her away to a far corner of the room before she realised what was happening, leaving Charlotte gazing after them thoughtfully, her blue eyes narrowed.

'What can I do for you, Mr Hawkton?' Josie forced all apprehension out of her voice but it was difficult not to feel intimidated by the big masculine figure in front of her. Being so tiny, she had never felt drawn to large, obviously virile men, preferring a slim, more aesthetic type of male to complement her slender fragility rather than a macho man, but she had certainly never felt *threatened* by a man's bulk before.

But it wasn't just that. It was something indefinable about him—insolent, challenging... And something in her own make-up, probably connected with the red hair, she thought with a silent spurt of amusement, was instantly antagonised as well as defensive.

'I came here today to see you.' The words hit her with a little shock that she had the sense to hide from the intent gaze.

'Really?' She managed a cool and, she hoped, very professional smile. 'With what purpose, Mr Hawkton?'

The hard mouth twisted in a small smile and she thought she detected approval in his narrowed eyes as he crossed his arms and leant lazily against the cream linen-covered wall behind him. 'You're very petite,' he said softly as his gaze wandered over the whole of her, from the top of her mass of curly red hair, tied high on her head in a restrained knot from which the odd tendril curled tightly, down to her small feet shod in expensive Italian leather court shoes that were nevertheless wonderfully comfortable and practical for a busy day like this one had been. 'Is that why you keep all that marvellous hair balanced on your head like that?'

'Not at all.' Keep calm; don't rise to his bait, she told herself flatly as she kept the smile in place by sheer willpower. Like most small people, she didn't particularly like her lack of inches being pointed out—and certainly not by a big brute like this man! 'I wear my hair like this because it is practical, Mr Hawkton, that's all,' she said quietly, with a touch of ice in her voice now that the sharp ears detected immediately.

'I've offended you. I'm sorry.' He straightened with a smooth twist of his body. 'You're sensitive about your height?'

'No, I am not.' She eyed him fiercely, her temper rising in line with the colour of her cheeks. What was it with this guy anyway? She had only known him for about sixty seconds and he was asking her the sort of personal questions even her closest friends wouldn't presume to ask.

'Good, because it's captivating,' he said surprisingly, and
there was a look in the silver eyes that told her he meant
exactly what he said. 'Quite captivating. Especially when
taken in conjunction with the red hair and beautiful eyes.
What colour *are* they exactly?' he asked as he leant down
and looked straight into her open gaze.

She snapped her head back as though she had been bitten,
narrowingly missing knocking a tray of glasses full of
champagne out of one of the waiter's hands. 'Look, Mr
Hawkton, I've got things to see to,' she said tightly, the
honey-gold eyes that he had admired flashing green sparks.
'I happen to be working here, and—'

'I know.' He didn't seem in the least put out by her abruptness. 'That's why I came today.' He smiled lazily.

'I—' She stared at him for a moment as her thought
process suffered a slight hiccup. Hawkton... Hawkton? She
knew she ought to know the name.

'But I mustn't keep you,' he said smoothly as he watched
and, she was sure, enjoyed her confusion. 'Perhaps we could
have a word later, before you leave?'

She nodded tightly. 'Of course. Now, if you'll excuse
me?'

His nod and amused, glittering eyes were an insult in
themselves, and she knew her cheeks were burning as she
turned from him. The creamy skin that came along with
the dark red hair showed even the slightest tinge of colour,
and there was more than a tinge today, she thought despairingly. She should have asked him who he was instead of
reacting to the conversation like a scalded cat. At least that
would have given her a clue to his identity.

She had a brief word with the catering staff to make sure
that the champagne would flow until the last guest left when
the doors closed at nine, checked that Evans, the security
man, was fully aware of all the arrangements, and then
signalled Penny to join her as she stepped into the office
behind the main gallery. They had only planned to be at
the opening for a brief hour or two, but a last-minute panic
had stretched out the hours.

'You go now, Penny.' Josie smiled at her assistant as she
joined her in the quiet office. 'You've put in more than

your fair share. And have a lie-in on Monday morning. I won't expect to see you until lunchtime. You've worked late every night this week.'

'Oh, thanks, Josie.' Penny smiled her appreciation as she reflected, and not for the first time, that she was very fortunate in having a boss as nice as Josie Owens. 'Are you sure you won't need me for the meeting tomorrow morning?'

'No.' Josie shook her head as she slipped off the desk on which she had been sitting and walked to the door. 'It's just a background fill-in on some new contract Mike and Andy are desperate to secure. I haven't even glanced at the bumph they threw at us all this morning.'

Mike and Andy were the co-directors and owners of the promotions firm, compulsive workaholics who were positively neurotic about snatching new deals from under the noses of their many competitors in the promotions field. Both men worked seventy- and eighty-hour weeks and expected their six executives, of which Josie was one, to do the same when necessary.

In spite of their extremely high salaries the other five executives, all men, considered themselves ill-used, but Josie didn't. Her work, her small circle of close friends, her beautiful flat in Chelsea and her cat, Mog, were her life. Fate had made it clear, thirteen years ago, that she couldn't expect more.

She and Penny left the office together and already the crowd had thinned. Josie signalled to one of the three art gallery staff that they were leaving and received a nod and a mouthed 'Thank you' from the middle-aged woman who would be in charge of the daily running of the place, and then she glanced round for Luke Hawkton. She would have to see him before she left, it would be too rude not to, but he didn't appear to be in the gallery.

And then she saw him, deep in conversation with Mr White, and, almost as though the power of her glance had drawn him, he looked up and straight over to where she was standing, and she knew, she just *knew*, they had been discussing her. But before she could react, think, even, he had moved swiftly across the space separating them and to her side, his dark face cool and blank.

'Do I take it you are available for that talk now?' he asked quietly with a polite nod at Penny, who nodded back, then made her goodbyes and left.

'Certainly, Mr Hawkton.' She had to raise her eyes some considerable way to meet the silver-grey gaze, and again the sheer breadth and height of the man sent something hot flickering down her spine, especially when her senses registered a whiff of the most delicious aftershave.

'Have you finished here?' he asked smoothly, his face quite expressionless.

'Finished...?' She looked sideways at him. 'I—yes, I've done all I can do—'

'Good,' he drawled, watching her with narrowed eyes. 'Then we can talk in comfort, perhaps? There is an excellent little Italian restaurant just a stone's throw away, so perhaps you would allow me to take you to dinner?'

'Dinner?' If he had said he wanted to take her to the moon she couldn't have been more surprised. 'B-but—' Oh, hell, she thought furiously, what was it about this man that made her stutter and stammer like a gawky schoolgirl? She had to pull herself together, and quickly. 'I'm sorry, Mr Hawkton.' She forced a cool smile and tried for the busy-career-woman brush-off that had always been so successful in the past. 'I'm afraid I'm busy tonight—'

'Rubbish.' It was said so matter-of-factly that for a moment the import of the word didn't register. 'Your able assistant—Penny, isn't it?—told me she had had orders to keep this evening free in case of any disasters here that needed sorting out. Now, I don't think you are the type of boss to tell the minions something like that and not do the same yourself. There are no disasters; you were about to leave... Need I go on?'

Disasters? If ever a disaster had been facing her this six feet plus of cold steel fitted the bill. 'I really don't think Penny had any right—'

'You are going to be difficult.' It was a statement, not a question. 'I don't like difficult women, Miss Owens; I don't like them at all,' he drawled slowly, his cool eyes assessing her so thoroughly that she could feel the heat from her skin like a brazier burning from the inside.

'Don't you, indeed?' Suddenly all the gloss and carefully nurtured aplomb of the last thirteen years took a nosedive. Who on earth did this man think he was anyway? She had never met anyone like him in her life before; he took the word 'arrogance' into another dimension! 'Well, perhaps what you like and don't like are not my problem, Mr Hawkton.' She smiled icily. 'And I was being quite genuine when I said I was busy. I have an important meeting tomorrow that I have to prepare for.'

'And you won't eat tonight?' he asked sardonically.

'I—' She bit back the hot words that were hovering on her tongue as she noticed one or two interested glances in their direction. Oh, this was ridiculous, crazy. She couldn't remember being put in a position like this since she was in her teens. 'Yes, I'll eat,' she said, with a calm that was purely surface level. 'Probably a sandwich, or something, while I work.'

'I see.' The silver eyes narrowed still more, and as he crossed his arms, his big chest formidable, she forced her eyes not to waver before his. 'What a daunting female you are,' he drawled thoughtfully. 'Do you frighten away the male population in general, or is it me in particular you have an aversion to?'

'Don't tell me I've frightened you, Mr Hawkton?' She managed a mocking smile.

'Oh, I wouldn't,' he assured her with wry amusement. 'In fact just the opposite, my fiery-haired little sprite. You see, I am a stubborn man, perhaps even inflexible and tenacious at times—' he smiled grimly '—and I have a reputation for always getting what I want. That might be a little exaggerated...' the narrowed eyes glinted ominously '...but only a little. And I have never been frightened by anyone, male or female, in my entire life.'

She could believe it. Oh, she could certainly believe it, she thought silently. Quite why he had caught her on the raw from the very first moment she had seen him she wasn't sure, but she was sure of one thing at least. *Everything* about him—his demeanour, the big, hard, aggressive male body, the aura of command and contemptuous authority—grated on her like a nail scratching down a metal surface and brought out the worst in her. It was unreasonable and certainly unfriendly but she couldn't help it. She didn't like him. She didn't like this Luke Hawkton at all, and she knew he knew it.

'Well, perhaps if you would like to tell me what you wanted to talk about?' she asked with studied politeness now, as the silence became so charged it crackled. 'I really do have to get home...'

'And I wouldn't dream of delaying you, Miss Owens.' He was annoyed. He was trying to hide it behind this mask of cool cynicism, but he was annoyed, she thought, with a moment of satisfaction she was immediately ashamed of. She imagined he didn't have too many women refusing an invitation to dine with him; it was probably a new experience for him and one he clearly didn't relish. 'Another time will do.'

'It will?' Suddenly, and quite irrationally, she wanted to know what he had been going to say. He wasn't the sort of man who would stage a casual pick-up; she was sure of that—besides which, he had already intimated that he had come to the opening of the gallery knowing she would be here. But how had he known? 'Who are you with?' she asked, with an abruptness she realised bordered on rudeness. 'Here—now?'

'Here—now?' He repeated her words with an insolent smile that had no warmth in its mocking depths. 'I am alone, as it happens. Does that matter?'

'But—' She gazed up at him, her creamy skin and dark red hair a wonderful foil for the wide honey-gold eyes with their emerald flecks. 'I sent out the invitations and—and your name wasn't there,' she continued bravely as the silver eyes iced over still more.

'True...' He clearly had no intention of embroidering on the one word of agreement, and she didn't know quite how to continue without turning it into an accusation. He must have had a special invitation, or been with someone who had, to get past the security set-up, she thought flatly. He must have... mustn't he?

'Would you like to see my credentials, Miss Owens?' With a little shock of anger she realised he was laughing at her, albeit silently; the gleam in the silver-grey eyes and the slight twist to the hard, firm mouth spoke of definite amusement.

'I don't think that will be necessary.' She tried for a coolness that didn't quite come off when matched with the fire in her cheeks. 'I'm sure you're bona fide—'

'How? How are you sure?' His tone was harder now, sharp. 'How do you know I'm not a terrorist, or some other undesirable who has tricked his way into this place? There's a hell of a lot of money on these walls today, after all— several paintings have been borrowed from private collections and are worth a great deal. How do you know I haven't been planning some sort of heist for weeks?'

'I—' Oh, help—he hadn't, had he? she thought, momentarily panic-stricken, before both the recollection of the security arrangements she had made and her natural common sense reasserted themselves. 'By several things,' she answered calmly as their glances locked and held. 'One, you are wearing one of the little metal tags we had made which are specially coded and numbered against the invitations.' She indicated a small narrow clip-badge on the lapel of his jacket. 'Two, there is only one way in through the front door today; the other door at the back of the gallery is bolted and alarmed and I checked it some time ago. And there are several other security precautions which it wouldn't be advisable for me to reveal that also make it impossible for anyone to gatecrash,' she added primly.

'Also, I have heard one or two people speak to you by name, so you are clearly known to them.' She hadn't meant to add that bit; it had just sort of slipped out. Now he would think she had been watching him, listening, and that was the last thing she wanted this mass of inflated ego to think, she thought irritably.

'I'm impressed.' The dark head nodded reflectively. 'Yes, I have to say I am quite impressed, Miss Owens. You are all they said and more.'

'All who said?' she asked quickly as her stomach tensed.

'Ah, now, that's another story, and you've already indicated your time is precious,' he said lazily. 'I mustn't keep you.'

The supercilious swine was certainly getting his own back, she thought tightly, but it didn't look as if his interest in her was on a personal level, as she'd thought at first. She waited for a feeling of relief that didn't materialise and put it down to the fact that she still didn't know why he *had* approached her.

'Goodbye, Miss Owens. I'm sure we'll meet again soon.'

He was leaving? And then, before she could do anything about it, he had reached forward and taken her small hand in his, raising her fingers to his lips in a brief salute that nevertheless reacted on her taut nerves like liquid fire as his flesh made contact with hers.

She was aware that she had snatched her hand away with more vigour than tact at the same time as he straightened, his face expressionless as he looked down into her hot eyes.

'Daunting...' The murmur was faint, but quivered with a dark amusement that made her want to kick him, hard, although she found herself frozen in front of him as the silver gaze held hers, merely staring up at him with large, expressive eyes. Then he bowed slightly before turning abruptly and leaving the gallery without a backward glance.

CHAPTER TWO

JOSIE found that she was frowning ferociously out of the window the next morning as she travelled to Hammersmith by taxi, a bulging briefcase and a wad of papers at her side on the back seat.

Luke Hawkton. *Hawkton*. She should have known the name but she just hadn't connected it with Hawkton Marine—not until she had got home from the gallery the night before, that was. She still remembered the shock of the moment when she had glanced at the data Mike and Andy had thrown at her earlier in the day, and realised she had just given the brush-off to one of the most powerful men in London.

'Luke Hawkton...' She groaned the name out loud as she twisted in her seat. But who in their right mind would have expected the illustrious head of the Hawkton empire to be at the opening of a small art gallery that he could buy and sell a hundred times over? she asked herself wretchedly. And she had dared to think he was actually interested in her as a person, that he was making a move on her!

She shut her eyes tightly as she remembered her cavalier treatment which had bordered on rudeness. That would teach her to keep her vivid imagination under control, she told herself bitterly. Oh, wouldn't it just! She'd had the opportunity of a lifetime, to sell both herself and the firm as the best thing since sliced bread, and she'd blown it.

The data from Mike and Andy stated that Hawkton Marine, one of the interests of the Hawkton empire first created by the present Luke Hawkton's great-grandfather, decades ago, were contemplating a grand-slam publicity extravaganza to launch their new yacht in the South of France later that year and were interested in hearing ideas from several promotions firms—of which they were one. Or had been, she corrected herself miserably, before she had put the proverbial boot in. Mike and Andy would kill her if they ever found out what she'd done. She opened her eyes as the taxi drew up outside the tall building in which Top Promotions was housed and gathered her things together quickly.

Once she had realised the enormity of her gaffe the evening before she had stayed up most of the night working on ideas for the publicity venture, her conscience searing all thoughts of sleep.

Mog had decided she was quite mad as she had paced the flat periodically, muttering and mumbling to herself, and he had finally retired, dignity and hauteur severely dented after she had fallen over him twice within as many minutes, to the comparative safety of the large sitting-room balcony, from which Josie had been quite unable to coax him in spite of the fact that it had begun to rain in the early hours.

He was clearly disgusted with her and she couldn't blame him, she reflected now as she walked up the wide steps to the building. She was disgusted with herself. How could she have missed such a gift of a chance to get in before their competitors? How could she? She glanced down at the briefcase in her hand, seeing in her mind's eye the photograph of Luke Hawkton that had been included in the data.

If only she had had time to glance through the information Andy and Mike had given her before she had left for the gallery the day before. But she hadn't. She shook her head as the lift took her swiftly upwards. All the regrets in the world, the sickening disappointment, wouldn't help now. Top Promotions would be the last firm, the *very* last firm Luke Hawkton would use. *Damn*! Damn, damn, damn...

'Josie...' Top Promotions occupied one floor of the large office block and as she left the lift, her small figure clad in a smart white linen suit and pale grey silk blouse that were both businesslike and feminine, she almost collided with Andy as he came shooting out of his office like a bullet out of a gun. 'Thank goodness you're here. Are Mitchell and the others with you?'

'No.' She stared at the elder of her two bosses in surprise. She had never seen him so agitated before. 'Should they be?'

'The *meeting*.' Andy took her arm as he hurried her along the corridor to Mike's slightly larger office. 'I told them eight-thirty sharp. Where the hell are they—?'

'Andy!' She shook his hand off her elbow at the same time as she came to an abrupt halt and glanced at her watch. 'It's only ten past eight now, for goodness' sake. What on earth is the matter with you this morning? What's happened?'

'It's Luke Hawkton.' For an awful moment, a breath-stopping moment, she thought Andy was going to tell her that Luke Hawkton had rung up to complain about her, but in the next instant she found her head against Andy's as he thrust his face so close to hers they could have been embracing. 'He's here.'

'Here?' Josie glanced wildly about the empty corridor. 'Where—?'

But before she could ask more Andy had taken her arm again and pressed her in front of him, reaching out and opening Mike's door as he urged her forward into the room and almost into Luke Hawkton's arms. He had clearly been standing just behind the door, and her urgent entry, aided by Andy's agitation, brought her to within an inch or two of the big, masculine body she remembered so vividly.

'Good morning.' The tone was deep and expressionless, but his eyes were wicked as they looked into her face, which she just knew was turning a deep shade of pink. 'You're obviously eager to start work, Miss Owens,' he said silkily.

'You know each other?' Both Andy and Mike spoke in unison, their faces quite unable to hide their hope at such an unexpected bonus, and Josie found herself struck dumb as she opened her mouth like a tiny stranded goldfish in the middle of a group of sharks.

'We've met briefly.' Luke Hawkton spoke smoothly and swiftly into the infinitesimal pause. 'I happened to be at the opening of the Duet art gallery yesterday which Miss

Owens was overseeing for this firm. My aunt is a great art-collector and had received an invitation.'

'But you said—' Josie had found her tongue, but not words in any coherent form, and as the silver-grey gaze turned back to her she found herself fighting the urge to turn and run. 'You said, yesterday—'

'Yes?' The word wasn't encouraging but she couldn't leave it.

'You said you were at the opening to see me,' she stated breathlessly. 'You *said* that.'

'And I was.' He eyed her unblinkingly, his mouth twisted in a cold smile. 'This latest project is very near to my heart, Miss Owens—the new yacht. My father died last year and it was he who first started the marine side of the business nearly forty years ago, always having had a great love of boats and water. This yacht was his own baby, if you like, something he had waited to see come to fruition for some time.

'Of course, the Hawkton name is second to none in the boat-building business, but this particular yacht is special, both to my family and myself. I want it to be successful—very successful.' His gaze now swept over the three of them and not one of them could have moved even had they wanted to.

'I always expect the best, Miss Owens, expect and receive it, and your name cropped up with monotonous regularity in my secretary's investigations regarding the best. Your name along with several others, I might add,' he finished drily, with a glance at Mick and Andy which warned them not to get too confident.

'I see.' It was all she could manage. She was stunned.

'And so I did my own investigations on each name and firm I had been given.' His eyes slanted on her pink face. 'And I discovered Top Promotions was owned—partly owned—by an old university friend.' He nodded at Mike, who returned the nod with eager enthusiasm, obviously anxious to make the most of the connection. 'Yesterday you were the last of three possibilities I have narrowed the field down to. The other two are excellent, incidentally...'

That's right, turn the knife a little more, she thought furiously as she kept her face pleasant with a superhuman effort.

'And what do you think of her work?' Mike asked earnestly. 'I'm sure you found Josie's reputation was well founded, Luke?'

'Are you?' The silver eyes were unreadable, which in itself was a warning for the 'old university friend' not to presume on their past acquaintance, and Josie held her breath, waiting for the Sword of Damocles to fall—although she had to admit there was more justification in her case than in that of Damocles, the poor courtier of Dionysius of Syracuse's court, who had had to endure a whole banquet underneath a sword suspended by a single hair, merely to prove his king's point that human life was insecure at best, irrespective of wealth or power.

The knock on the door in the next instant was an answer from heaven, and she could have kissed Mitchell and Tony as they filed into the room immediately afterwards, necessitating the normal social introductions during which Mike's question was forgotten.

The other three executives were in their seats by eight-thirty, and as the meeting commenced and the ideas flowed Josie tried to relax. But it was no good. That big, dark, masculine figure on the other side of the room was stilling her normally vivacious tongue and paralysing her thought process. She knew Andy and Mike had glanced at her more than once, clearly expecting something from her, but she was quite incapable of responding to the silent order.

It was her own fault, she thought desperately. She knew all this was her own fault, but did Luke Hawkton have to be so... so *satisfied* about her predicament? He had her on the end of a hook, he knew it and she knew it, and every time she nerved herself to meet the silently superior narrowed gaze she knew he hadn't forgotten or forgiven her for yesterday's confrontation.

So what was he going to do about it? she asked herself helplessly. Tell her bosses she had messed up? Denounce her in ringing tones and watch her squirm? Well, whatever he was going to do she wished he would just get on with it, that was all. She couldn't take much more of this nightmare of a meeting without disgracing herself still further.

And then, almost as though he was receiving her unspoken thoughts, he leant across the large desk around which they were clustered and spoke directly to her, his voice deep and soft. 'Miss Owens? Perhaps you would like to show us your ideas now?'

No—no, she wouldn't, but she couldn't very well say so. She knew he was going to pick them all to pieces, exact a revenge that would be satisfying for him and painful for herself, but there was absolutely nothing she could do about it. She was in the ultimate catch-22 scenario, and the most galling thing of all was that she had put herself there.

'Certainly.' She avoided his intent eyes as she lifted her briefcase onto her lap and extracted the night's work. 'I've tackled the concept from several different angles, actually, as I wasn't sure how formal or glitzy you wanted the launch to be. Now, this was the first idea I had . . .'

As she talked the different possibilities through her enthusiasm for the work she loved took over, as always, her voice steady and firm now and her face animated.

'And this is my last thought . . .' She lifted her eyes for a moment as she spread the papers out in front of Luke Hawkton and her gaze met the piercing force of his. She faltered slightly before quickly recovering herself. 'I wasn't sure if there would be children present, or whether you wanted an evening reception strictly for adults, but this idea could encompass both if you so wished.

'I thought a play on old and new might capture jaded imaginations better than a straightforward diamonds and fur occasion, and with that end in mind I considered going back a hundred years or more for the day. Perhaps an old-fashioned fair, complete with rides and swings and so on, and a constructed ice-rink with braziers and roasting chestnuts?

'Everyone invited could wear clothes suited to that era, the children could have hoops and kites to play with, and the climax to the launch could come at the end of the afternoon, before the formal dinner dance planned for later, with several small boats in the harbour providing coloured smoke to form a veil through which the new yacht can sail, beautifully streamlined, utterly gracious—the present in all its glory...

'The dinner dance later could either be a seventeenth- or eighteenth-century ball, complete with crinolines, or an up-to-date affair to allow the women to show off their Diors and so on—with, of course, champagne on the yacht first for the selected few.' She nerved herself to glance up and look directly at Luke Hawkton as she finished speaking, but the cold, rugged face was completely expressionless, the silver-grey gaze hooded and remote.

As the seconds ticked by she was aware that everyone was waiting for some sort of reaction from the man himself, as was she, but nearly a full minute passed before he broke a silence which had become electric.

'Excellent.' The glittering gaze lifted from her rough sketches and calculations to fasten with steel-like firmness on her face. 'We'll go with that last one.'

He had risen, pushed back his chair and was halfway across the room before anyone moved, and then Mick and Andy shot out of their chairs like startled rabbits. 'Luke, do I take it we've got the promotion?' Mike asked breathlessly, his voice a tone higher than normal, and the other men rose from their seats like obedient marionettes, leaving only Josie sitting in stunned silence at the deserted table.

'No.' Luke turned, his silver gaze flashing over his old college friend like liquid steel. 'Miss Owens has.' He smiled directly at her now, the hard face mellowing for a moment. 'I like the general theme you've suggested—it's both unusual and imaginative—but I want to be kept closely involved with this—you understand me?'

She nodded dumbly, unable to believe that Top Promotions had just scooped what must be the prize of the year.

'And I don't want other ideas fuzzing the edges.' The gimlet gaze returned to Mike. 'No interference from other ambitious avenues, right? I'm aware you work as a team here on most projects, but not this one. I will provide Top Promotions, and Miss Owens, with both the finance and resources to give me exactly what I want. The launch will be at the end of October, which is two months later than I would have liked, but our team of craftsmen ran into difficulties with the original superstructure moulding and it needed modifying.'

As Mike and Andy's heads moved in unison Josie wondered, for a split second, exactly what Luke Hawkton was thinking as he watched them all. He was powerful, hard, ruthless, wealthy; he had just given their company an enormous shot in the arm and he must be aware of the fact, and of the exalted position that put him in in her two bosses' eyes. Did he expect obsequiousness, servility from his employees? She had dealt with enough egomaniacs in her time to know that some men looked on such things as their right.

'Today is the second of June.' The deep voice brought her fully alert. 'That means you have almost five months to pull this off. Can you do it?'

He was looking directly at her again, and she nodded tightly without a shred of hesitation. Either that or die in the attempt!

'Good. And can I also take it that you will obey any instruction I give you regarding the project without question?'

This time her hesitation was marked, and she nipped at her lower lip for a moment before finding the nerve to speak the truth. 'No, not if it isn't in the best interests of the launch or if I think you're wrong,' she said honestly. 'In those circumstances I would want to discuss things with you and see if we could arrive at a mutually agreeable solution.'

She saw Mike and Andy, who were standing just behind Luke now, close their eyes for a split second, but in spite of their horrified faces she continued to stare into the silver-grey gaze without flinching. She had never toadied to anyone, man or woman, and she was blowed if she was going to tell Luke Hawkton a pack of lies. She wasn't a boot-licker or a bosses' lackey; she had a mind of her own and knew how to use it, so he might as well know now.

'Daunting...' The word was breathed on the air but she read his lips, and the memory of her rebuff the day before brought vivid scarlet into her cheeks. 'I would like you at my office on Monday morning with some relevant facts and figures,' he continued immediately, his voice cool, as though his reference to her gaffe had been incidental. 'If you have any other projects under way you delegate them to one of these gentlemen. You can agree with that, Miss Owens?' he added with heavy mockery.

It clearly didn't make any difference whether she was happy with his orders or not, but she nodded anyway, her large honey-gold eyes still faintly dazed by the suddenness of it all. 'Thank you.' She hadn't meant the words to sound so small or so breathless, but somehow the sheer presence of this man had drained all her normal vivacity into a small, trembling lump in the middle of her chest, although there was no reason for it, or for the hostility that flared into life every time she so much as laid eyes on him. And she *was* grateful for this wonderful opportunity. 'Thank you, Mr Hawkton.'

'You're welcome.' He walked back to shake her hand, and as he did so he spoke swiftly and softly in her ear, his voice inaudible to the others. 'And you've managed it without having to use that couch at all. Unfortunately.'

He had turned and left before she could pull herself together sufficiently to think, and then, as the door closed behind him with Mike and Andy glued to his heels, her colleagues were congratulating her somewhat grudgingly and the remark had to be put on the back-burner of her mind.

'So Mike was at uni with the esteemed Luke Hawkton, was he?' Mitchell was obviously put out that his ideas hadn't had a mention. 'Think that's why he's going with Top Promotions?'

'I think Josie's proposal had something to do with it,' one of the other men remarked drily. 'Don't be a sore loser, Mitch; it doesn't suit you.'

But Mitchell's comment, along with Luke's parting shot, were in the forefront of her mind that afternoon as she sat in her comfortable, bright lounge with the full-length windows to the balcony wide open and Mog lying in purring

ecstasy in a spot of blazing sunlight with a whole cel-
ebratory tin of red salmon in his stomach.

It was Luke's 'unfortunately' that bothered her, more
than the fact that he had referred to her stupid gibe to
Charlotte. He surely hadn't taken her seriously, had he?
She bit on her lower lip anxiously as she went over and over
the intonation of his voice in her mind. But so what if he
had? She could handle that sort of hassle; she'd been doing
it for ten years or more, since she'd first stepped out into
the big bad world. But she wouldn't like to think she'd got
the job because Luke happened to know her boss.

She frowned into the thick warm air. He either genuinely
liked her ideas or he didn't. And if he didn't . . . She shook
her head slowly. How did you know with a man like him?
He wasn't like any other man she had ever met in the whole
of her life . . . except one. The thought jumped in from nowhere but once in her mind it stuck.

Yes, there *was* something about him that reminded her
of Peter Staples, something . . . something she couldn't quite
put her finger on, and it had caused an instant and probably
unfair antagonism that was as fierce as it was illogical. She
thought back to her behaviour of the evening before and
winced at her barely concealed hostility to the man who
was now, in effect, her bread and butter.

'Oh, Mog . . .' She sighed as she spoke but Mog was too
full of salmon and too comfortable to respond to the naked
appeal in her voice. He cast her a long, considering glance
from large, slanted green eyes before the express train in
his chest resumed its rumbling journey, the sunlight turning
his brindled fur into a mass of shimmering colour.

This was the chance of a lifetime, an opportunity to nail
her colours well and truly to the career mast and cement
her credibility into place with unshakeable firmness, and
she wasn't going to let Mitch's spitefulness or Luke
Hawkton's innuendoes spoil things. She narrowed her eyes
determinedly, pushing back the riot of tiny auburn curls
that fell about her shoulders. She could do it. She *knew*
she could pull this off; that wasn't in question. The only
thing was . . .

Her mouth hardened. Could she tolerate Luke Hawkton in her life for any amount of time? The thought was stupid and she knew it. Of course she could; she would have to. And he wasn't Peter Staples; he wasn't even remotely like him.

Peter had been wild and dark and fascinatingly handsome to the young fifteen-year-old Josie Owens, with his long jet-black hair and slanted ebony eyes that danced wickedly as they promised the moon. He had been ten years older than she and quite out of her orbit, with his flashy red sports car and his succession of tall, model-type girlfriends that he seemed to change with each passing month.

Their parents had been friends, but then everyone was friends with everyone else in the tiny Sussex village where she had grown up. And so she had loved him from afar, utterly tongue-tied if they ever happened to meet at one of the numerous social gatherings the middle-aged community loved so much and which the younger folks tended to endure, watching him with huge doe eyes and hanging on his every word.

Quite when he had started to flirt with her she wasn't sure. She had heard rumours that his last girlfriend, a sophisticated, leggy blonde with the face of an angel and the figure of a goddess, had thrown *him* over—an unprecedented occurrence—and that he was upset about it, but she hadn't been able to bring herself to believe the hearsay. Who in their right mind would reject Peter Staples? He was . . . just perfect. And so when he'd told her to keep their dates secret she hadn't asked him why. One didn't question a god.

They had seen each other three times before he had made the pass at her which had ended in an undignified fight for her virginity. She could still hear the caustic, ugly words he had shouted at her in the heat of his temper when he'd realised his crude seduction attempt had failed, the foul language as he had pulled her back into the car, furious that she had refused him and was demanding to go home.

And then he had driven like a madman, the more so when he had seen her fear, and the car had seemed to fly down the narrow, high-bordered lanes with their tight curves and bends, its expensive tyres screaming and the world outside a green blur. He had been laughing when the car turned the corner and hit the farm tractor.

It had been the first thing she remembered when she had finally come out of the coma—that spiteful, malevolent laughter ringing in her ears and the crash of grinding metal against metal.

The young eighteen-year-old farmboy had been killed instantly; Peter had walked away from the crash with nothing more than cuts and bruises. And she...? She had had a fractured skull, two broken legs and a crushed pelvis that had necessitated an operation. An operation that had robbed her of the chance of ever being a mother.

'Stop it, Josie.' She spoke the words out loud and this time something in her voice brought Mog to his feet, and he stretched comfortably before sauntering over and rubbing against her legs. 'Good boy...' She spoke automatically, her hand stroking the sleek fur as she gave herself silent orders to pull herself together.

Trips down memory lane were futile and destructive; she knew that. She *knew* it. And it was rare for her to indulge in them these days. The ringing of the telephone at her elbow interrupted her self-admonishment.

'Miss Owens?' Luke Hawkton's voice was unmistakable.

'Yes?' Her heart stopped, and then raced on like a runaway train.

'This is Luke Hawkton. I'm sorry to bother you at home like this but I have a problem.'

'You do?' Oh, for goodness' sake say something businesslike, something that will impress him, she thought disgustedly as she heard her faint, breathless voice.

'I have to fly to Germany tonight—an unexpected business complication that may well necessitate my spending several days out there.' The firm, controlled voice wasn't unfriendly, but nevertheless she found herself holding her breath as she listened to him. 'I don't want any further delay on the *Night Hawk* project, Miss Owens; there has been enough already. The thing seems to have picked up problems like a cat picks up fleas.'

'Oh.' She glanced down at her feet to meet Mog's bright green gaze, which she was sure had darkened with disapproval at his simile.

'I would like you to get all the relevant data sorted out over the weekend and bring it out to me. I will arrange for a car to pick you up at eight on Monday morning and my secretary will be waiting for you.'

'I...' She took a deep breath and tried again. 'Are you saying you want me to fly out to Germany, Mr Hawkton?'

'The name's Luke, and, yes, that's exactly what I'm saying,' he said coolly.

'But I could fax you—'

'No, that would not be satisfactory.' He cut across her protest immediately. 'I want you in front of me, where we can discuss things properly and get everything ironed out,' he continued firmly. 'Your plane leaves Heathrow at nine-thirty, so I understand, and my secretary will give you the tickets and all the necessary information concerning your hotel and so on. A car will be waiting on your arrival in—'

'Hang on a moment, did you say hotel?' She found her voice along with her wits, and at the same moment it hit her why Luke Hawkton reminded her so strongly of Peter.

They were the only two men she had ever met who were completely and totally sure of themselves and of their ability to command, to subdue, to dominate. It sat on them like a live aura and both repelled and fascinated those unfortunate enough to come within striking distance—or at least it repelled her now, she thought bitterly. Thirteen years too late.

She would always believe it had been Peter's utter lack of remorse, his unwillingness to accept any blame for the accident or her injuries, that had caused her father's massive heart attack. In the two months before he died her father had been eaten up by bitter pain and resentment that his only daughter had been treated so badly, and he had felt her desperate anguish and primitive blind despair as though it were his own. On the day before she'd finally come out of hospital he had collapsed in the street just outside the main doors and died moments later.

'Just an overnight stay, Miss Owens—or may I call you
Josie? As we are going to be working pretty closely over
the next few months I think a less formal approach is called
for, don't you?' The deep, faintly husky voice broke into
her thoughts, commanding her concentration.

'Yes, of course.' She forced a pleasant tone that was in
direct contrast to her feelings. 'But with regard to the hotel
I'm sure that isn't necessary. I can easily catch a night flight.
In fact, I'd prefer to do that,' she added firmly. 'I have
things to do here—'

'Which I am sure can wait twenty-four hours.' There was
a touch of steel in the pleasant tone now, only the merest
intimation that his words were an order and not a
suggestion, but it was enough to make the hand holding
the phone clench tightly round the inoffensive instrument
as she glared at it angrily.

'I'm not sure exactly when I will be free to talk to you,
so it makes sense to allow a little leeway into the evening.'
His voice was reasonable—too reasonable, as though he
were explaining something obvious to a recalcitrant child.
'You do understand the enormity of the job you have taken
on, I trust?'

'I think so, Mr—' She stopped abruptly. She couldn't
call him Luke, she just couldn't, but he would think she
was being awkward if she insisted on Mr Hawkton. 'I think
so,' she repeated carefully. 'And of course if you'd prefer
me to stay over then I will. You're the boss.' She had wanted
the last three words to sound light, but they had merely
sounded petulant.

'That I am, Josie,' he said quietly, his voice very dry.
'Now, a car will be at the entrance to your block of flats
at eight on Monday morning with my secretary, Emma,
inside. All you need to bring is your passport, an overnight
bag and, of course, the details on the project. I have informed Mike and Andy of the arrangements, incidentally.'

I just bet you have, she thought tightly, before giving
herself a mental slap on the hand. What was the matter
with her, for goodness' sake? The man was going to spend
a small fortune on this damn launch; he had every right to
expect her one hundred per cent commitment. 'That's fine.'

She injected a note of enthusiasm into her reply. 'I'll see you on Monday, then.'

'Goodbye, Josie.' Was that thread of sardonic amusement always in his voice, or had he guessed the extent of her reluctance? she thought tightly. If he had, he had clearly taken great delight in commanding her obedience. Oh, stop it, stop it, she told herself desperately. She had to take hold of this unwarranted hostility to a man she knew nothing about and bring logic and reason to the situation.

Luke Hawkton was a respected, powerful multi-millionaire, with business interests in more concerns than most of London put together. He had chosen her proposal, *hers*, not Mitchell's or one from the other firms he had checked, and there was everything to thank him for. *That* was fact. These... feelings of hers were irrational, unjustified and in the circumstances downright dangerous if they began to jeopardise her professionalism.

With the benefit of hindsight she could see that Peter Staples had been a wastrel of the first order, a spoilt, vain megalomaniac with something base and vile at the bottom of him—a man who was actually unable to feel any sense of remorse or contrition. He had stood in court after the accident and lied so convincingly, and with such conviction, that if she hadn't been in the car herself *she* would have believed every word he'd spoken. He'd got off scot-free, or as near as dammit, and had walked away from the whole mess without a thought for the two dead men and the ruined life—hers—that he'd left behind him.

But... She shut her eyes for a moment as she bit on the underside of her lip, her teeth nibbling agitatedly at the soft flesh. But there was still *something*—the enormous confidence, perhaps, the unswerving faith in their own ability and power—that linked the two men in her mind.

Peter Staples had changed the course of her life, her whole future at fifteen. His cruelty had turned her into something dry and desolate, her body into a barren place that would forever be unfruitful, empty. They had all told her she was lucky to be alive, that she had so much to be thankful for in that the only scars she had didn't show, but they didn't *know*. They didn't understand how it felt to be in her head, to know that she was a woman on the outside only, a mutilated shell irrevocably flawed.

She had refused to go to counselling sessions after a few weeks; the motherly little woman with a photo of her grandchildren on her desk hadn't helped much. And then had followed a period of blackness, deep, primitive blackness, from which she had eventually pulled herself inch by inch when her mother had become ill just as she had started her two-year college course. Nursing her mother and coping with her extensive studies had left her with no time to brood on her dark thoughts, and on the night her mother had died she had made a vow to herself.

No chasing rainbows, no hoping for the moon, no happy ever after. She was on her own now, and on her own she would remain. She would never ask any man to accept second best. She had raised her chin proudly and stared into the mirror through eyes drenched in tears. Her career would be her life and she would go for that one hundred per cent.

It wasn't the life she would have chosen, but her options had been ripped out of her with the surgeon's knife. There would be no romance in her life; she couldn't risk getting close to someone only to shatter their hopes. No, she would make the best of what she had. She *would*. And cut the self-pity from that moment on.

And she had. Almost. She opened her eyes and stared round the pretty, well-furnished room. She was very, very fortunate. *She was*. And this chance now to go still further was welcome, marvellous.

But in spite of Luke Hawkton's munificence, in spite of the fact that he had been nothing but generous so far, she didn't like him. Illogical, unreasonable, absurd—yes, it was all that and more, but nevertheless something linked him in her mind with Peter Staples, and she couldn't do anything about it.

CHAPTER THREE

'JOSIE. How nice to see you again. I trust you had a good flight?' The deep, dark voice trickled over her nerves like liquid fire.

'Fine, thank you,' she responded carefully.

As Luke took her small hand in his, his large fingers swallowing hers whole, she forced herself to betray none of the agitation that had gripped her as soon as he had stridden into the hotel's small conference room.

On arriving in Germany, she had been met at the airport by an impressive limousine that had swept her in style to the luxurious first-class hotel where she was to be staying. There she had been greeted with a deference that had left her nonplussed, until she'd realised she had come under the umbrella of Hawkton Enterprises.

Her room was the last word in opulence, the lunch that had been provided five minutes after her arrival simply superb, and the ground-floor conference room that had been reserved for her alone had meant she could spread out all her countless pieces of paper and continue working in comfort while she waited for the great man to put in an appearance.

And now he was here. And he looked very, very big. The beautifully tailored suit and grey silk shirt and tie he was wearing sat well on the hard male body, but couldn't disguise the muscled strength in the broad shoulders and chest. He was uncompromisingly virile, in fact menacingly so, and again that strange little shiver of sensation snaked down her spine as she felt his warm flesh against hers.

'You have been busy.' In spite of the fact that he had let go of her hand almost immediately, the burning memory of his hard hand gripping hers remained with her for several seconds before she could erase it and bring her mind under control sufficiently to reply.

'Yes.' She nodded with what she hoped was cool aplomb. 'I've sketched out a few rough ideas on different angles for the fair and the ball later. There's a Victorian look, or perhaps you'd prefer an Edwardian style? And we need to determine pretty early on whether the period you choose for the fair will run over into the ball, because if so your guests will need some considerable time to get appropriate clothes ordered for both. The ice rink will be expensive to construct, of course, and we will have to provide a vast number of boots in different sizes—'

A discreet knock at the door broke into what was fast becoming a gabble, even to her own ears, and a second later a waiter entered, carrying a tray containing coffee and cakes.

'Thank you.' Luke's voice was cool and calm, and once the waiter had left, leaving the tray on the table at their side, where Luke had indicated it should go, he turned to her, a slight smile curving the hard mouth. 'Do I make you nervous, Josie?'

'What?' The word escaped before she could draw it back, and she knew she was blushing a bright red as she qualified it hastily. 'No, not in the least. Of course not.'

'Of course not.' He repeated her words with slow, laconic disbelief, his dark eyebrows slightly raised as he leant back in his chair to survey her through narrowed eyes. 'There is no need to be nervous, I do assure you. You have the job. It is, as they say, in the bag.'

'I know.' If only it was just the job in hand that was the trouble, she thought silently. If only. 'And there's no problem, really,' she said brightly, willing the hard, astute man in front of her to believe the lie.

'Good.' The piercing silver eyes remained trained on her face for one more moment before they dropped to the papers in front of him and he waved his hand at the tray. 'Would you care to be mother?'

It was an old phrase, and one that she had come up against many times in the last few years, but it still had the power to hit her in the stomach like a hard fist and she was glad that that glittering gaze was no longer on her.

'Milk or cream?' she asked carefully as she poured the coffee.

'Black, please.' He didn't look up as he spoke. 'And I'd like a piece of that disgustingly rich fruitcake while you're about it. Lunch seems a distant memory, and I can see we'll be tied up here for an hour or two. Dinner at eight suit you?'

'Dinner—?' She stopped abruptly. She somehow hadn't expected to have dinner with him, although, thinking about it now, maybe she should have. But she had supposed he would be busy with other high-flying tycoons—the ones he had come out here to see, presumably.

'You do eat?' he drawled quietly, still with his eyes on her work.

'Yes.' In spite of all her good intentions—and she had been repeating them to herself ever since waking very early that morning—her stomach clenched in protest at his faintly mocking tone. 'And eight would be fine.'

'The food here is more than adequate, but I know a little restaurant that is excellent if you don't mind a drive?' The devastating gaze swung to her face before she had time to school her features into an acceptable mask, and she saw his eyes narrow as they fastened on her tight mouth.

'I don't mind—really,' she said hastily. 'Whichever you'd prefer.' She passed him the coffee and cake as she spoke and then almost dropped the plate as a tingle shot up her arm at the touch of his fingers.

If he noticed her little start of surprise he said nothing, accepting the coffee and cake with a polite word of thanks and then transferring both his gaze and his energies to the job in hand.

And Josie found, after a few seconds had slipped by, that the razor-sharp mind and intimidating intelligence of the man in front of her called forth all her powers of concentration—so much so that she was absolutely amazed when, some time later, Luke glanced at his watch and announced that two hours had slipped by.

'I think we've covered the initial groundwork.' He smiled at her as he stretched with animalistic grace, his hard muscles flexing under his clothes. 'Certainly enough to give the thing a kick-start, anyway.'

She nodded quickly in reply, forcing a polite smile to her lips. He had been absolutely right, of course. There was no way the majority of this could have been sorted out by faxing or telephone calls or anything else. It had needed a one-to-one discussion; she had been stupid to suggest anything else. As it was she was going to have her work cut out to keep to the schedule they had drawn up; every day, every hour would count from now on.

'Let me take those.' When she'd finished packing all her sketches and papers into her large black briefcase and leather folder he took them from her, tucking them under his arm as though they weighed nothing at all. 'Your room is just down the corridor from my suite. I'll call for you at eight and we'll drive to that restaurant, OK? I'd like a decent meal after the last day or so.'

He gestured for her to walk through the door he had just opened, and as she did so the realisation that she was being controlled by a superior force, one that represented danger, was so strong that she could taste it. And along with that disturbing knowledge came the fact that she was vitally aware of every single movement of that big, powerful male body, that she had been even when immersed in facts and figures and calculations. Even then her subconscious had registered every slight gesture, every action, however small. It was humiliating, mortifying, but her mind and body seemed determined to respond to this man in a way she couldn't control, and she didn't like it at all.

The first few months after the accident had been a dark nightmare as she had struggled to come to terms with the loss of her father and also the end of all her girlish dreams of marriage, a husband, babies. *Babies*. For a time it had seemed as if the whole world revolved around babies. Every television commercial, every programme or magazine featured wide-eyed infants, be they black, brown or white, and each one had screamed her deficiency at her, the fact that she was hopelessly, irreversibly flawed.

Babies had become a terrible and wonderful fascination for her, a whip with which she beat herself daily, an obsession she couldn't overcome. She had spent hours in front of a mirror with a cushion in front of her stomach under her clothes, the tears streaming down her face as she had cried her desolation from the black void where her heart had been.

But then, slowly, she had begun to claw back her mental stability, forcing herself each morning, minute by minute, hour by hour, to count her blessings. She had become nurse as well as daughter to her mother, and in a strange way that tragedy, following so hard on the heels of the accident and her father's subsequent death, had settled her emotions. She hadn't had time to dwell on her own grief as she had sought to make her mother's last days happy ones, and unbeknown to herself it had been therapy for them both.

When her mother had died she had been almost seventeen, but she had felt like an old, old lady as she had determined the path her life would follow. A fulfilling and interesting career, and a destiny that she and she alone would control, with no emotional or romantic commitment of any kind. Her parents' death, coming so soon after Peter's cruel treatment of her adolescent adoration and its devastating conclusion, had turned the word 'love' into something that meant agony, misery, suffering and bereavement.

She had determined to be strong, mentally and physically. *She* would be in control of both her emotions and her fate from now on. No more being tossed about by the waves on the sea of life; no more crying for what had been taken so brutally from her. She would make her place in a world in which children rarely featured and learn to be content with that. She *would*.

And now? She was aware of Luke just a step behind her as they walked to the lift. Now, for the first time in all those years, that control had been shaken. And she was having dinner with him tonight! Was she mad? Before she had time to consider her next words, she turned round so sharply that he almost walked into her.

'Mr—Luke, I really think I would prefer to have a meal in my room tonight,' she said hastily to the dark, hard face above her, stumbling slightly over his name, which seemed as though it had burnt her lips. 'It will give me a chance to go over a few of those calculations, and I'm really very tired . . .'

She found her voice dwindling away as he stood looking down at her, his silver-grey eyes gleaming in the dull artificial light overhead and his face perfectly still. Even when he wasn't speaking, perhaps *especially* when he wasn't speaking, the cold, compelling aura of the man was fiercely strong.

'You don't lie very well—unlike most of your sex, I might add,' he said thoughtfully after a few tense moments had passed. 'You'd really find my company so hard to take?'

'I— It's not that. I'm just—'

'Tired?' He cut into her red-faced mutterings with cool composure as the lift doors glided silently open, and she knew her legs were trembling slightly as she stepped into the carpeted box. 'Josie, you are twenty-eight years of age and as free as a bird—no demanding husband in the background, no little infants hanging on your coat-tails and interrupting your sleep, not even a live-in lover, from what I can determine. You are young, beautiful and healthy, right?'

The glittering gaze was as sharp as finely honed steel as it swept over her and the lift doors slid shut. 'Now, in view of all this are you seriously trying to tell me that you are so exhausted you can't make dinner tonight?'

'How do you know all that?' She forgot the matter of dinner as she glared at him across the small space, anger competing with the warning her brain was giving her to go steady, to keep cool. 'All that about my personal life.'

'Is it inaccurate?' He was leaning against the lift wall as he spoke, muscled arms crossed over a broad chest that wouldn't have disgraced a prize wrestler.

'That's not the point,' she replied hotly, her face burning as she frowned up at him, her tiny, delicate frame taut and her honey-gold eyes flashing green sparks. 'My private life is nothing to do with you or the job.'

'Don't be so ridiculous,' he said coolly.

'Ridiculous?'

'Yes, ridiculous.' Now the hard face had set into pure granite, and there was a chill emanating from the silver-grey gaze trained on her face that could have frozen molten lava. 'Hawkton Enterprises is a large and varied organisation, as I'm sure you are aware, but as I think I explained to you Hawkton Marine is particularly important to me.'

Because of his father? Yes, she remembered as the lift deposited them at their floor, the doors gliding open to reveal a hushed, scented corridor with ankle-deep carpeting and hothouse blooms perfuming the still air.

'The person I chose for the Night Hawk project needed to be mentally and emotionally on the ball—a quality that can't always be determined at first glance,' he added cynically. 'I had no intention of employing someone with a messy or complicated private life, and if that offends you— tough.'

'So you spied on me?' she asked in disbelief, her voice high.

'*Spied* on you?' he asked, in a voice that resembled splintered ice. 'I control Hawkton Enterprises, for crying out loud, not the Secret Service. You've been reading too many novels, young lady. I merely made enquiries as to whether you were free to put in the number of hours this job would entail or whether there were personal ties in your life that would make it difficult. If you had had a husband and children you would have seen little of them over the next five months, and although that may be fine during the initial euphoria it very quickly palls, believe me.'

'And you'd have made the same enquiries about a man?' she asked tightly as they came to a halt outside her door.

'Most certainly.' He looked at her steadily. 'I don't go in for sexual discrimination in any shape or form. I've been accused of many things in my life, but chauvinism is not one of them. Could you say the same?'

'What?' His question had taken her completely by surprise and it showed.

'You don't date—or very rarely. You have a circle of a few close friends, none of whom are male. And you have a way of looking at me with those huge golden eyes as if I was something that had just slithered out from under a stone,' he drawled sardonically. 'It doesn't take a genius to work out that for whatever reason the male animal is a species you find less than trustworthy.'

'Oh, really?' She couldn't remember when she had been so mad. 'I'm surprised you didn't apply the age-old male explanation for all that.' She had meant her tone to be scathing, but it wasn't quite so forceful as she would have liked. His intuition had frightened her, badly. She had been right to feel he was dangerous. 'That I must prefer women? Isn't that what you men usually assume when your egos are dented?'

Part of her couldn't believe that she was having this conversation with the head of Hawkton Enterprises, that she could well be throwing away both this particular project and the job she had worked so hard for at Top Promotions. If he fired her now—and he could, easily—Mike and Andy would be livid with her.

'I have no idea what men do when their egos are dented, Josie; such an . . . unpleasant calamity has not befallen me to date.' He smiled easily, his equanimity quite unaffected by her all too obvious rage. 'But it sounds painful,' he added drily. 'Now, can we stop this childishness and agree on dinner at eight?'

She immediately thought about arguing some more, but somehow the instruction didn't get through to that part of her brain which governed her responses, because she found herself nodding dazedly as he took the key she had been holding and inserted it in her door, pushing her gently into the room beyond and shutting the door after her.

She stood for some minutes in the quietness of her room before her hand reached for the light switch. Immediately the room was bathed in a soft golden glow from the carefully positioned lighting, and the thick cream carpet and curtains and pale lemon furnishings appeared both tasteful and restful to her tired eyes.

He was generous; she had to give him that. This must be one of the best rooms in the hotel, after all. She shook her head gently as she ran her hand across her face in a quick, confused gesture that spoke of her inner turmoil. He had probably wanted her easily available if he needed to consult her about anything, and his suite *was* just down the hall... This was all to suit him, that was all it was—

'Stop it.' She swallowed painfully after speaking out loud into the silence. It didn't matter whether he was generous or not. The only thing of any importance was the *Night Hawk* project. Once that was completed she would have had a terrific boost to her career prospects, an undreamed-of advance up the ladder of success.

And this feeling she had had of late—that it was all futile, empty, that she wanted more, someone to call her own, something to love—well, that was just a classic case of the grass being greener—human nature in all its perversity. Because she had no choice; she had no choice at all, did she? Her options had all disappeared thirteen years ago on a beautiful summer's evening in June amid a mass of tangled metal and burnt rubber.

'You look quite beautiful.' It wasn't so much what he said as the husky deepness in that rich voice that made her heart beat a trifle more quickly as she opened the door to Luke just before eight.

She was dressed simply but expensively in a sleeveless cocktail dress of russet silk, the wafer-thin straps over her shoulders and softly fitted bodice showing the creamy perfection of her skin to its best advantage and the three-inch heels on shoes of exactly the same shade giving her petiteness a small boost. She'd left her hair loose, and it fell in tiny shimmering curls about her face and shoulders, accentuating the fine, heart-shaped face and huge golden eyes.

'Thank you.' She managed a light smile, but the way the black dinner jacket sat on those massive shoulders had given her a nasty moment. He oozed sex appeal—positively *oozed* it, she thought helplessly as her mind went blank on the conversation front. And she didn't like the warm ache that his male sensuality called forth from the core of her; it was crazy, stupid. She wasn't attracted to the he-man type, not remotely. *Not remotely*, she told her quivering nerves.

'All ready?' His voice was impersonal now, and she nodded quickly before stepping past him into the corridor and shutting the door firmly behind her.

Ready? No, she wasn't ready, she thought nervously as he put a casual arm round her waist and guided her into the lift, which was waiting at their floor, his flesh burning hers through the silk of her dress.

Once in the lift, she moved carefully to one side, turning to face him as she strove for nonchalance. 'You've stayed here before?' she asked lightly.

'Several times.' If he noticed her manoeuvre to avoid his touch he gave no sign of it, his voice pleasant and untroubled. 'When you travel as much as I do, if you find a good hotel you stick to it, believe me. I like good food, swift service and most of all a comfortable bed.'

This time she refused to let herself blush at what was a perfectly normal conversation after all, although there had been an inflexion in the dark, deep voice that she was sure she hadn't imagined.

'Yes...' Come on, blind him with some riveting repartee, she told herself angrily, but the flagrant masculinity showed no signs of abating, and it had the unwelcome effect of stilling her normally quick tongue. It didn't help that it was completely natural either...

He had to be one of the most attractive, sexy men she had met in a long time, she realised suddenly with a shock of surprise. Women must adore him. 'I really think the launch is going to be the most talked about event for years,' she began quickly. 'I'm sure—'

'Josie?' he interrupted her softly, his voice lazy. 'You aren't working now.'

'But—'

'No buts.' His eyes glinted at her, daring her to argue. 'Don't you ever relax?' he asked silkily.

As they reached the ground floor and the lift opened onto the luxurious reception area she smiled coolly, her back straight. 'Of course I relax,' she said tightly. 'Often.'

'When?' he challenged quietly.

'What?' She stared up at him as he brought her to a halt by turning her to face him, his large hands under her elbows.

'When do you relax?' he asked patiently, his voice soft. 'Really relax, I mean.'

'I... All the time.' Was he flirting with her? she thought nervously. She really didn't know. But what she did know was that the coldly intimidating, ruthless tycoon had metamorphosed into the perfect dinner companion, and of the two she found the latter infinitely more alarming. 'When I'm at home—'

'By yourself?' There was a dry, mordant note in the lazy voice now that immediately grated on her nerves. He turned from her, taking her arm and leading her into the small cocktail bar just off Reception.

'There's nothing wrong with being by yourself,' she said hotly, stung into temper. 'Besides which I have lots of friends, and my cat—'

'Josie, old ladies of ninety have lots of friends and a cat,' he drawled, with inexcusable amusement. 'Now, our table at the restaurant isn't booked until half-past nine, and I'd like you to try a particularly delicious cocktail here before we leave. I'm sure you'll love it.'

'What's it called?' she asked tightly, her temper still at boiling point but unable to do anything about it with the attentive barman hovering in front of them as though Luke were royalty.

'Chaste Delight.' He raised one sardonic eyebrow at her as he spoke. 'Although I rather think that is a contradiction in terms... Good evening, George.'

The silver gaze turned to centre on the barman not a moment too soon as her urge to kick him became almost overwhelming. 'How's your wife?'

'Getting along nicely now, Mr Hawkton, thank you,' the barman said, with a deference that Josie found intensely irritating in the circumstances. 'We've roped the grandparents in to help out a bit; they love it and it gives Frieda a break.'

'Good idea. All hands to the plough—or in this case three ploughs.' Luke glanced at her with a wry smile. 'George's wife recently gave birth to triplets; they don't do things by halves over here. That'll teach you to marry a big, healthy German girl, George,' he continued smoothly as Josie forced herself to smile politely. 'If you'd stayed in the old country you wouldn't have had this problem.'

'No problem, Mr Hawkton.' The other man grinned cheerfully. 'You want to see the mugshots?'

'Do I have a choice?' Luke returned wryly but with a warm smile. 'And while we do that perhaps you'd mix a Chaste Delight for the lady, and I'd better have a mineral water, George. I'm driving.'

Josie steeled herself for what was to follow but it still hurt; it always did. Three little cocoons with tiny faces exposed to the camera in the arms of their proud parents. *Three*. She kept the smile in place with gritted teeth. It wasn't fair. Life just wasn't fair.

'They're very sweet.' She handed the photographs back to Luke as though they had burnt her, and George busied himself with serving their drinks before disappearing to the other end of the bar as another couple wandered in.

'Did I detect a note of boredom there?' Luke asked softly as she took a long, deep swallow of her frothy pink cocktail to quell the trembling in her stomach.

'Boredom?' She was immensely glad of the kick in the drink as she raised purposefully blank eyes to his. 'No, not at all.'

'Do you like children?' he asked quietly.

He had no idea what this conversation was doing to her, and she drew on every scrap of strength she had won over the last few years and answered flatly, her voice even, 'I suppose so. I don't really come into contact with any.'

'The original career woman?' There was a note in his voice she couldn't quite place, but his face was relaxed and pleasant. Nevertheless she felt he disapproved of her, of the negative reaction he had sensed and misunderstood, and it hurt. It was stupid, crazy, but... it hurt.

'You don't get to the top by playing happy families,' she said levelly.

'No, I guess you don't, at that. But you sure as hell miss a lot if you don't.' He stared at her, hard, for one more moment before indicating the drink in her hand. 'Finish that and we'll have another before we leave.'

She didn't normally drink—alcohol of any description always went straight to her head—but tonight she downed the drink in one swallow and held out her glass to Luke with a devil-may-care soreness in her heart.

He thought she was an ambitious career woman, hell-bent on getting to the very top of the tree? Well, maybe she was. In any case it was an impression she had deliberately fostered through the last few years, hiding behind a mask that protected as well as concealed, so she couldn't very well blame him now if he believed it.

She sipped the second drink slowly; the first cocktail already doing peculiar things to her head. Or was that Luke's presence? she asked herself as she smiled at some witty, dry remark he had just made. He was all charm tonight, but the dark, formidable side of him was still just a breath away, and she realised suddenly that he would be an intimidating adversary to deal with in business—or anywhere else for that matter.

And there was still that cool, easy assurance about him, the utter belief in his own power, that reminded her of Peter. It repelled her even while she couldn't deny the little trickles of excitement shivering down her spine. And from the covert glances that had been thrown in their direction from more than one or two pairs of female eyes it appeared she wasn't the only one to be affected, either.

As she finished the last of the pink liquid he smiled at her, his eyes slightly narrowed as they washed over her small, beautiful face and moist lips. 'Shall we go?'

He took her arm as they walked out of the hotel and she took a deep, silent pull of the warm summer air, but it did little to steady her nerves. You are in control. You *are* in control. She repeated the refrain over and over in her mind, and by the time she was seated in the large, sleek car with that big, powerful male body in close proximity she had restored a little of her faltering equilibrium.

'Nice car.' She needed to say something to break the tension that was so tangible she could almost reach out and touch it.

'It is adequate,' he said with cool smoothness.

Was he *really* so calm and composed? she asked herself as the engine growled into life. It was intensely aggravating that she was reduced to a nervous wreck while he was the original ice-man. But then everything about Luke Hawkton was aggravating, and being alone with him like this was the last thing she had wanted.

There was something about him—something...primitive. The word shocked her, but the more she rolled it around her mind, the more she knew that it fitted the cultured, sophisticated man next to her, in spite of the layers of civilisation that sat so powerfully on the dark frame. In the intimacy of lovemaking, when exploring the secrets of sensual delight, he would be primitive...

She jerked herself away from the dangerous path her thoughts were following with a physical movement as she chastised herself harshly. What did she know about it anyway? she thought bitterly. She was hardly an authority on the subject of men! She didn't know what made Luke Hawkton tick; she didn't have a clue. And what was more she didn't want to know either. She kept that assertion to the forefront of her mind throughout the long drive and the necessary social chit-chat, and when they arrived at the secluded and very exclusive restaurant she steeled herself for the evening ahead as though she were going to her doom.

They were shown to their table with all the ceremony normally accredited to royalty, and the head waiter appeared like a genie as they sat down. Although the conversation was in German, Josie was aware that the power of the Hawkton name was well known as the tall, middle-aged man clicked his fingers at the wine waiter, who glided to their side.

'White or red?' Luke asked her smoothly.

It was on the tip of her tongue to say that she rarely drank either and would prefer a glass of iced mineral water when some perverse sense of pride reared its head. 'Red, please.' She smiled brightly. In for a penny, in for a pound. If she was going to give a performance as a hard-bitten career woman she would need help from somewhere, and she was loath to reveal anything of the real Josie to this man.

'Red it is.'

When yet another waiter handed her the ornate menu she was immensely thankful to see that it was printed in

German, French and English, although even so most of the dishes were unknown to her.

'The lobster and avocado salad is very good here.' He spoke after she had been eyeing the list for a few moments, his voice casual as he kept his eyes on his own menu. 'And perhaps I could suggest the fricassee of veal to follow, with sauté potatoes, honeyed pineapple, carrots and creamed mushrooms?'

'That sounds very nice.' She nodded her approval, and as Luke spoke swiftly to the waiter in rapid German the wine waiter came back, his face wreathed in smiles as he poured a small amount of what was clearly a very expensive wine for Luke to taste.

Once they were alone again she forced herself to speak lightly as Luke settled back comfortably in his chair, his strange silver-grey eyes narrowed on her face. 'You speak excellent German.'

'Thank you.' He bowed his head briefly in a gesture that was curiously Latin. 'My nanny was German, my father English and my mother Italian, and we had houses in France and Italy as well as England so I was speaking several different languages at an early age without even thinking about it.'

'A privileged upbringing.' No wonder he had such a big opinion of himself, she thought silently. He'd probably been treated like a little prince from the day he was born.

'Yes, it was.' She had tried to keep her voice even and without expression but as his mouth tightened she felt he had sensed her criticism. 'I was most fortunate. But even the comfortable blanket of enormous wealth can't still fate's hand.

'My twin brother died when he was just fourteen. Leukaemia,' he added abruptly. 'So although I might have been a spoilt little brat up to that point I then grew up very quickly.' His voice was cold now, and stiff. So he *had* discerned her disapproval, she thought as a wave of guilt and shame turned her cheeks scarlet. What could she say now?

'I'm sorry.' She looked him full in the face and didn't try to pretend. 'I'm very sorry about your brother and for jumping to conclusions. I had no right to do that.'

'No, you didn't.' His gaze was holding hers very tightly and then he relaxed suddenly, his eyes crinkling as he smiled, *really* smiled, for the first time since she had met him. The result was devastating.

Did he *know* what that warm openness did for him? she asked herself in stunned disbelief. The way it mellowed the hard, rugged features and softened the piercingly keen eyes? He wasn't just attractive, he was... Well, he was...

'But there's no need to look so tragic; you had no way of knowing about John. And for the record we weren't spoilt, not much anyway. My father was a great disciplinarian and my mother, like all Italian women, ruled her house with a rod of iron.'

'All of them?' She smiled as she spoke and he laughed right back, his chuckle appreciative.

'All of them,' he confirmed, just as the waiter arrived with their lobster and avocado salads.

The rest of the evening passed in a warm haze of good food, delectable wine and a mixture of conversation and laughter. The lobster was delicious, the fricassee of veal in its sauce of cream, lemons, herbs and onion was mouth-watering, as were the accompanying vegetables, and the coffee soufflé Josie chose for dessert was so light she thought it would float out of the dish.

It was as she was finishing the last luscious spoonful of soufflé that alarm bells began to go off in her head like clanging cymbals. In fact it was just as Luke leant across the table and touched her cheek gently with one finger before tracing a path to her mouth.

'I can't remember when I enjoyed a meal so much.' His voice was deep and resonant and did something incredible to her stomach.

'I thought you said you'd eaten here often?' she parried lightly.

'I wasn't talking about the food.' She felt her face flood with colour, and at the same time she realised she was way, way out of her depth. He was an accomplished man of the world, ruthless in business and probably in his private life too, and wealthy—no, not just wealthy, filthy, disgustingly rich—and he'd probably had more women than she'd had hot dinners.

He thought she was a hard career woman who had willingly chosen to pursue her vocation at the cost of marriage and a family, and who just happened to be without a man at the moment. In his world it would probably be the normal thing for her to pop into bed with him, and then they would enjoy a brief affair until either one of them tired of the fun. No strings, no recriminations, nothing heavy.

But she wasn't like that. What would he do if she told him she was a virgin? The thought brought a brief surge of hysteria that she squashed immediately. She shouldn't have let herself relax so completely, enjoy herself so much. It was those cocktails and then the wine. And him. Definitely him.

'Well, I thought the food was wonderful,' she said, with a careful coolness that was quite at odds with the mad pounding of her heart. 'Thank you very much for the lovely evening.'

'You are very welcome.' His voice was grave but slightly mocking as his piercing eyes wandered over her flushed cheeks and anxious mouth. He settled back in his seat again, his big body relaxed and his face cool and sardonic. 'Would you like coffee here, or perhaps it would be more comfortable back at the hotel?'

'I think here would be nice,' she said primly as she tried to fight both the cloudy effects of the alcohol she had imbibed far too freely—first in panic and then because she simply hadn't realised what she was doing—and her own feelings of attraction for the man sitting opposite her.

And she *was* attracted to him. It was a relief to finally admit it, and with the acknowledgement came the realisation that she had been fighting just that very thing since the first moment of laying eyes on him.

What was it with her anyway? she asked herself with grim ruefulness as she nerved herself to look into the silver-grey gaze trained on her hot face. Had she got a death wish or something? Even an experienced, worldly coquette like Charlotte Montgomery, who changed her men along with her nail varnish, would have trouble handling this man.

'Here? You're sure?' He smiled slowly, and she had to admit it was a devastatingly sensual technique that would make most women melt. But she nodded firmly as she smiled a polite if unknowingly nervous smile. 'Here it is, then ...' He didn't seem at all put out, and although part of her was relieved that he had accepted her decision so gracefully a tiny part of her, unawakened until this very moment, was piqued.

The easy conversation and laughter of the meal was a thing of the past as they sipped their coffee. Josie's whole body was as tight as a coiled spring and Luke was sardonic and mordant when she answered his efforts at conversation with monosyllables which if they weren't exactly rude came very close to it.

She was aware that she was handling this whole thing extremely badly, and conscious of the fact that he must be wondering what the hell was going on, but she had never been more frightened in her life. She had let her guard down, for the first time in the whole of her adult life, and she didn't understand why or how she could be so physically attracted to a man she had only known a few days when she had had no trouble of that kind in the whole of the last thirteen years.

They left the restaurant with the head waiter virtually bowing them out, his face wreathed in smiles, and although the man's obsequiousness wasn't Luke's fault Josie felt as angry with him as though it were.

'What's wrong?' They had been travelling in silence for some miles, and when Luke spoke Josie jumped visibly before she could control herself.

'Wrong?' She forced a bright smile that was wasted on the man sitting next to her as he concentrated on the dark, unlit road through the windscreen. The restaurant had been situated in rolling countryside—part of its appeal, Luke had assured her when she had spoken of it during the meal— and they were now travelling through what looked like farmland on a lonely road that she remembered from a few hours ago was almost devoid of other traffic. 'Nothing's wrong.'

'I don't believe you.' The deep voice was perfectly calm. 'You were enjoying yourself there for a time during the meal, weren't you? What is wrong with that?'

'Nothing—'

'And then you scuttled back behind that inch-thick armour with almost indecent haste,' he continued mockingly. 'Even fierce career women are allowed a few hours off occasionally, or hasn't anyone told you?'

He thought her retreat, which on reflection *had* been a little obvious, was down to her concern about her image? She wasn't sure whether to be relieved or vexed that he considered her so shallow. Vexation won, and her voice was sharp when she spoke. 'Do you really like going to places like that, where you are made such a fuss of?' she asked tightly. 'Is that sort of thing important to you?'

'You think I took you there to make some sort of impression?' he asked, with a silky note to his voice that fooled her for a moment, until she glanced at his hard profile and the straight line of his mouth. 'Is that what this is all about?'

'I didn't say that.' Oh, hell, why hadn't she kept her big mouth shut? she thought despairingly. She was going to look an idiot however this conversation went.

'I see. So you were just enquiring as to my ego level for the sake of social intercourse?' he drawled derisively. 'Your own special type of after-dinner conversation, I presume?'

'I... It...' She'd been right; she was looking an idiot. The knowledge provided the burst of adrenalin she needed to bring her stammering voice under control and straighten her back against the leather seat. 'Mr Hawkton—'

'I don't believe we're back to Mr Hawkton.' She could have hit him for the laconic amusement deepening the cool voice.

'Luke,' she amended hastily. 'I didn't mean—'

'Don't lie to me, Josie.' Now there was no humour tempering the silky steel. 'I've been lied to by experts, who have had immediate cause to regret it. You have me down as an egotist, the type of man who is so full of his own importance, so self-absorbed, that he finds it necessary to flaunt his assets at every opportunity, to rely on the suspect admiration of dependants to boost his credibility with a beautiful woman. That was what you meant...'

He paused, and she found she was holding her breath. 'No doubt you have met a considerable number of such sad people in the world you and I inhabit. The rat race is fierce, with everybody using their wealth and power to guard their space, making them easily prone to corruption. I *am* aware of that, and also that a beautiful woman like yourself must have been propositioned more times than she can remember.'

She didn't say anything; there was nothing to say.

'But I play the game of life by my own rules, Josie, and I've never had the need to bribe or coerce a woman into my bed.'

The hard, sensual face turned to her for just one second, and she shivered at the aura of pure masculinity that was so sexually attractive it hurt. Bribe or coerce? she thought with a faint touch of hysteria. He probably had to fight them off in droves.

She was just about to make a suitably defusing type of reply, to get the conversation back on a more neutral level, when they rounded a corner in the dark country road to find several large cows standing stolidly in their path, their big faces turned towards the car's headlights. She was aware of Luke swearing grimly at her side at the same moment as he swung the car into the grass verge, the brakes screaming as the car nosedived into the long, shallow ditch beyond. Her seat belt clutched her as she jerked forward, the engine made a harsh tearing sound, and then all was quiet besides the disconcerted mooing of the disturbed bovines.

'Are you all right?' Luke turned to her instantly. 'Are you hurt at all?'

'I don't think so...' She hadn't had time to think, it had all happened so fast, but now the memory of that other crash thirteen years ago turned her legs to jelly and his face began to blur in the moonlight.

'You aren't going to pass out. *Josie*...' He undid her seat belt as he spoke roughly in her ear, before opening his door and moving round the back of the car to the passenger side, whereupon he almost dragged her from her seat into the mild night air. '*Josie*, take some deep breaths. Come on . . .'

It was the fact that she was enclosed in his arms, rather than any medicinal properties in the slight breeze outside the car, that put a surge of feeling where faintness had reigned, enabling her to stand upright instead of sagging against the hard wall of his chest. 'I'm OK . . .'

He didn't let her go immediately and she was painfully, vitally aware of the muscled strength of his chest through the thin silk shirt he was wearing. His jacket was open and hanging either side of her as his arms continued to enclose her softness. 'There's no rush. Take some deep breaths and relax; you'll be fine,' he murmured softly against her hair.

Not with you holding me like this, I won't, she thought ruefully. Relaxing and being held next to Luke Hawkton's body weren't compatible. 'Really, I'm all right now.' She forced a smile as she raised her face to look up at him, in an effort to reinforce her words. This was the present; the past was dead and gone, she told herself firmly.

His eyes held hers for a few endless moments, glittering silver in the darkness of his face, and then he lowered his head, brushing her lips in a light, tantalisingly light caress as he carefully put her to one side. 'I'd better inspect the damage in that case,' he said quietly.

She hoped, oh, she did *so* hope that he was unaware of what that brief embrace had done to her, the way it had reduced her to a quivering mess inside, while he . . . He was the original Mr Cool.

She watched him now as he raised the bonnet of the car and bent over into murky blackness. 'I can't see a damn thing in here,' he muttered after a few seconds had ticked by. 'I don't suppose there's such a thing as a torch in this hire car.'

'Do you want me to look?' she asked quickly. Anything would be a relief compared to the racing of her thoughts. She *knew* the embrace and brief kiss had been nothing more than an effort to comfort on his part, that he would have done the same to any female, and she didn't like the way it had affected her.

'No, don't worry.' He straightened, his outline big and dark in the moonlight. 'There's no way I'm going to be able to get this thing out of the ditch tonight, so it's immaterial whether the engine's survived or not. Stupid animals...' He turned his head to survey the cows, who had fled back into the field bordering the other side of the road via a hole in the wire fence they must have escaped through earlier and were lumbering away into the darkness.

'Won't...won't we need a torch to see our way?' she proffered tentatively as he moved back to her side.

'Where exactly are you thinking of going?' he asked lazily, a faint smile twisting his lips. 'There's nothing for miles except fields and grass.'

'But we can't stay here.' She pushed a shaky hand through her tumbled hair and then wished she hadn't as the narrowed eyes watching her so closely slanted still more, indicating that he had noticed her trembling.

'No?' he said indolently. 'Is there something I'm missing? Why can't we stay here, Josie?'

He knew. He *knew* what he did to her and he was enjoying this, every moment of it, playing with her like a cat with a mouse. How dared he? *How dared he*? Her chin came up, her mouth thinned and her body tensed for battle. 'Because we could be here all night if no one comes along. It's very lonely—'

'Isn't it?' he agreed laconically.

'So we have to try and get some help,' she persevered, hanging onto both her temper and her dignity with severe difficulty. This was her employer...like it or not. And she didn't. She certainly didn't.

'Do I take it the panic in your voice is caused not so much by a fear of the dark, or wide-open spaces and large animals, that sort of thing, but more by the thought of a night in close proximity to me?' Luke asked with deceptive softness.

'Not at all.' Her chin tilted even higher, but he was completely still as he stood there looking down at her diminutive shape, and she couldn't read a thing in his dark face. 'It's just that I've some work to do when we get back, that's all.'

'Work. Yes, I see...'

'And you must be very busy,' she continued desperately, her heart fluttering like a captive bird at his quiet scrutiny. 'I'm sure you're in a hurry to get back.'

'Strangely, no...'

He was going to kiss her. As the dark head lowered she knew she ought to protest, to make some movement to repulse him, but she found herself rooted to the spot as he curved a powerful arm round her shoulderblades and drew her against his muscled chest, so close that she was enfolded in the delicious smell of him that had been titillating her senses for the last few minutes.

She closed her eyes, her head falling back instinctively as her lips parted, but after a few seconds she opened them again to find him staring down at her, the silver gaze narrowed and inscrutable, and then he whisked her off her feet and deposited her back inside the car.

'What...?' She must have spoken out loud, because when he joined her a few moments later his dark face was mockingly satisfied.

'You were getting wet feet out there.' He indicated her sodden shoes with a flick of his head. 'I thought you would be more comfortable in here,' he said smoothly as he glanced her way.

'Did you?' she said flatly, and her face burnt hotly. He had known she expected him to kiss her, damn it; he had engineered that whole little episode to make her look foolish. And she hadn't even noticed she was standing in two or three inches of water. How could she not have *noticed*? What had all that been anyway? A lesson to teach her that he could take or leave her? Was that it? Retribution for the panic he had sensed earlier?

His next words seemed to confirm her suspicion.

'You're quite safe, Josie.' He tugged his bow tie loose as he spoke, leaving it hanging either side of his collar as he undid the first two buttons of his shirt, the result of which sent her senses into overdrive as the sudden informality hit her like a fist in the chest. 'It's been years since I seduced a date in the back of my car. I prefer more...comfortable surroundings these days.'

'I'm not a date,' she said, more breathlessly than she would have liked.

'Exactly.' The silver eyes glittered for a moment. 'So you are doubly safe, yes?'

'I never thought my safety was in question,' she said with forced lightness.

'Good. In that case you will understand my reasons for not taking you on a route march across the countryside in the vain hope that we'll stumble across some habitation,' he said lazily. 'We have no idea where the nearest house is, and, romantic though the moonlight is—' he cast a mocking glance at her hot face '—it's not conducive to midnight rambles. Twisted ankles or broken legs are not on my agenda for this trip, OK? Now, some late-night traveller might well come across us before morning, and the farm vehicles are out at dawn—'

'And failing that we follow the cows home for milking?' she said brightly, determined to act as though a night spent with Luke Hawkton didn't bother her an iota.

'Just so.'

He smiled that slow, sensual smile that had the power to turn her inside out, and she gulped deep in her throat as she lowered her head, allowing her hair to fall in a veil across her burning face.

'In spite of the beautiful weather I don't think that dress is going to be warm enough...'

To her horror, her utter horror, he shrugged off his jacket as he spoke, the thin silk of his evening shirt accentuating the massive shoulders and muscled chest more effectively than nudity would have done. She could see dark body hair curling on his chest where his shirt was undone, and, as her hands went damp and her mouth went dry, her blood heated to fever-pitch and she shut her eyes tightly.

'Thank you.' Her voice was a squeak as he placed the jacket over her, and immediately the warmth and smell from his skin enveloped her with the dark material, causing her lower stomach to tighten and throb.

'You're very welcome.'

His voice was grave and she didn't dare glance at his face, keeping her eyes shut as she settled into the car seat, feigning tiredness. In fact she had never been more awake in her life, every nerve, every sinew screaming for release. She kept absolutely still for several minutes until he spoke again, his voice silky and cool in the darkness.

'Cows I can take, and even the fact that I've put the car in a ditch in the middle of nowhere and there's an important call coming through from Canada to the hotel at midnight doesn't bother me too much, but what does annoy me is the fact that you're as rigid as a board. What the hell do you expect me to do to you, for crying out loud? I thought I'd reassured you that rape isn't my style?'

Josie turned slightly and looked at him carefully, trying to make her face as blank as possible to combat the brilliant colour staining her flushed cheeks. 'I don't know what you are talking about,' she said tightly.

'No?' His eyebrows expressed his disbelief as they moved into a harsh frown. 'Lady, you're so nervous you'd have *me* believing I was the Marquis de Sade if I didn't know differently.'

'I'm not nervous.' She glared at him now as her temper was fired. 'I was merely thinking about what we discussed today, running over a few ideas in my mind.'

'As your employer, I can only applaud such conscientiousness.' His voice was expressionless but she sensed sarcasm, although the dark, rugged features were giving nothing away, his eyes hooded and indolent as he looked back at her. 'You aren't the average sort of businesswoman, are you?' He shifted in the seat slightly as he spoke, obviously finding its tight confines too restricting for his big body, and she tensed at the movement before forcing herself to relax.

'You don't think so?' she asked quietly.

'No. No, I don't think so,' he said softly, repeating her words with musing mockery. 'You're so tiny, for a start, so delicate and...breakable. How the hell do you survive in the jungle we inhabit anyway?'

'I don't think my part of the jungle is anything like yours.' She wanted to turn away from him, to drop her eyes from that glittering gaze, but it mesmerised her. 'I just do my job the best I can, and I enjoy it, of course—that helps.

And I'm quite tough, actually; appearances can be deceptive.'

'I'm well aware of that,' he said with deep cynicism. 'Believe me, I learnt that at a very early age, courtesy of the sharks and barracudas on two legs who would sell their own grandmother for a quick dollar.' He turned fully to her now, lifting her chin with a thoughtful hand, and she forced herself to remain perfectly still at his touch. 'So you're tough, are you? A thoroughly modern woman of the nineties who knows exactly where she is going and what she wants?'

'Yes.' She stared back at him steadily. 'I've got a good job, a lovely flat and I enjoy my life. What more can anyone ask?'

'Someone to keep you warm in bed at night?' He spoke lightly, but at her tight shrug his eyes narrowed. 'Most women have a nesting instinct, don't they? An urge to settle down eventually?'

'I've no idea.' She forced a smile. 'But then I'm not "most women". I'm an individual—me.'

'That wasn't meant disparagingly,' he said quietly. 'But even the most determined career women often combine home and family with a job, and very successfully, too.'

'Yes, they do.' The smile was brittle now. 'But it's not something I would want to put myself through, frankly. I've seen some of those "determined" career women desperately trying to juggle home commitments, a sick child, a difficult husband, and all the time wearing themselves to a frazzle. It isn't worth it.' She lowered her chin as she spoke, forcing him to withdraw his hand.

'So it's one or the other?'

'For me, yes.' She wanted to brush a loose curl off her cheek, but didn't dare extract her hand from under Luke's coat, knowing he would see the trembling she was trying to hide. Why couldn't he just leave her alone? This conversation was killing her; she was pretending to be something she wasn't.

'Let's hope you don't regret it when you're an old lady and other moguls have taken your place,' he said shortly.

'I won't.' She tried, she really *tried* to keep all bitterness out of her voice, but those sharp ears must have caught something, because there was a long moment of silence and then his voice was soft when he spoke.

'What was his name, Josie? And don't tell me it wasn't a man who soured you to thoughts of settling down and family life.'

'I prefer my job. What's wrong with that?' she fired back tightly.

'I don't believe you,' he said calmly.

'Well, it's probably not good business sense to argue with the boss, but this time you've got it wrong.' She raised her face and looked at him, which was a mistake. His eyes were fixed on her and a bolt of electrical awareness shot between them, its impact devastating.

'As I've said before, you aren't a very good liar, Josie Owens,' he said softly. 'And that, along with several other things, doesn't quite fit in with the image.'

'I've no idea what you're talking about—'

The last thing, the very last thing she had expected at that precise moment in time was his kiss. His head lowered in one heartbeat as he leant over her and then his mouth was on hers, warm, coaxing and unbearably sweet.

She couldn't believe it for a second, her mouth stunned beneath his, and then as her heart began to pound wildly she was aware of the delicious sensations of touch and taste as he drew her close against him. His lips were sensual and knowing and so, so sure, and the kiss deepened and held until she knew he must feel the trembling she couldn't control.

The angle of his body was pressing the soft fullness of her breasts against the hard wall of his chest, and the rippling warmth from their tender, engorged peaks was heightening what his mouth was doing to her, causing the blood to surge through her veins with an excitement that was almost unbearable. He was an expert, a virtuoso at this... The thought was there, but too remote to make any impression on her entranced state.

And then, with an almost cynical disregard for her melting capitulation, he adjusted her head against his shoulder as he settled more fully into his own seat again. 'Now that should be more comfortable...'

She heard the words above her head without their impact registering for a few seconds, and then, as she realised that he was asking nothing more, she felt burning colour start at her toes and fire upwards into every part of her body.

'Use my shoulder as a pillow and bring your feet up into the seat. You're so tiny it's like a bed to you anyway.'

He'd stopped. *He'd stopped*? She did as he suggested simply because her body had gone into automatic as her mind exploded with the knowledge that he was totally unaffected by the kiss. Those few minutes had been the most devastating of her life and he was as unruffled as always, composed and untroubled.

But he must have known how she felt, sensed her response... She bit her lip so tightly she was aware of the salty tang of blood in her mouth. Or had it all been a subtle kind of punishment for her thinking the worst of him? The same kind of thing she had sensed earlier, when he had lifted her into the car? Was he teaching her a lesson, showing her that he could have her compliant and docile in just a few minutes if he put his mind to it?

She almost groaned out loud. Because he could... Damn him, he could. Oh, this was ridiculous. Of course he couldn't. It would only have been a few moments more before she would have pulled away. *Of course she would*.

'Warm enough?' His voice was deep and cool and she could quite cheerfully have hit him for its steadiness. She managed a nod against his shoulder, not trusting her voice, which she was sure would be as shaky as the rest of her, and then everything else was forgotten as he began a rhythmic, soothing stroking of her hair. 'Try and get some sleep. It's been a long day and you must be exhausted.'

Exhausted? If the circumstances had been different she would have laughed out loud at the incongruity of calling her throbbing, volatile body 'exhausted'. There was a heat, a furore inside her that she had never experienced before, and she didn't have a clue how to handle it.

But then, as the minutes passed and she remained lying against him, the touch of his hand on her hair light and calming, she began to relax and her mind dulled. She couldn't think any more; it was too tiring... She was too battered, too confused...

CHAPTER FOUR

A DOCTOR, returning from an emergency call to an elderly patient, found them just after two, and by three Josie was back in her hotel room, lying in the warm, scented darkness, trying to force her mind back into the slumberous blankness she had felt in the car. But it was no good...

She watched as dawn began to weave streamers of gold and pink and mauve into the night sky, and then rose impatiently, padding through to the luxurious *en suite* bathroom and standing under the shower for a full ten minutes while she struggled to come to terms with her shattered emotions. As the warm, silky water splashed a velvety path over her face and body she gave herself a mental dressing-down that was all logic and sense—and didn't help an iota.

Her *brain* knew that Luke Hawkton was a brief hiccup in her life, that the devastating kiss and embrace in the car had meant nothing to him beyond a wish to comfort and reassure her in the unusual circumstances in which they had found themselves. Reason and sense added that she was just the same person she had been for the last twenty-eight years, and that she and she alone controlled her destiny.

He probably wasn't remotely, faintly interested in her anyway, not with all the sophisticated, worldly and undoubtedly beautiful women who had and still did grace his life and his bed. So why, when her mind knew all that, did she feel as though she was on a collision path with a brilliant black meteor that had a momentous power to ravage and destroy?

'Stop being so stupid...' She spoke out loud as she folded one of the massive fluffy bathsheets round her, her fingers absently tracing the thin silver scar on her stomach that was all that visibly remained of the horrific accident that had almost taken her life.

She pulled back the towel as she walked through to the bedroom, pausing in front of the large full-length mirror and forcing her eyes to concentrate on her body, her gaze dissecting and ruthless.

The surgeon had been careful to do a good job. The scar was as low as he had been able to make it, flat and thin, barely noticeable now after thirteen years. Yes...he had done a good job and had undoubtedly saved her life in the process. She nodded slowly at her reflection. And she was grateful to him for that, very grateful, although she hadn't been at the time.

Later, after her mother had died, she had gone back to the hospital to thank him properly for his skill and expertise, and most of all for his kindness to her when she had been less than appreciative. She still remembered the words he had spoken to her as they had sat in his office, bright sunlight spilling over his grey head from the window just behind him and his eyes full of compassion.

'I'm not going to pretend that your sense of loss at what might have been will ever completely fade, Josie, but I do know you will learn to accept what you can't change. In the initial days after the accident, when you were still in the coma, we tried everything we could to avoid taking such a drastic step, but the internal damage was too severe and surgery was the only option.'

She had nodded her understanding, her heart too full of pain and regret to allow her to speak without breaking down.

'Your parents knew what it would mean to you. They told me that since you were a toddler you'd adored first dolls and then babies, anything younger than yourself. Some girls, women, could adapt to their changed circumstances, but you will never fully do that; you'll learn to live with it instead, you understand?'

She had nodded again, more vigorously this time, thankful that he hadn't parroted the empty platitudes she had heard so often in the last few months from well-meaning neighbours and friends.

'You have your eyes, your ears, your intellect, and a body that is healthy and young. It is up to you what you do with these gifts, but, knowing you as I do, I don't think you will let them go to waste. You have lost something irreplaceable, Josie, and the grief will always be there. To mourn is natural, my dear, but life has a way of compensating if you'll let it.'

'A way of compensating.' She pulled the towel tightly around her and sat down at the dressing table as she began to dry her hair. Yes, she had been doing all right in this adult-populated world she had carved out for herself. No, not had been, *was*. She wouldn't let it be any other way. It was up to her, Luke Hawkton or no Luke Hawkton.

'Good morning.' When Luke surfaced from behind his newspaper as the waiter pulled out her chair he gave no sign that he remembered the happenings of the night before in either his face or his voice. She had expected some form of awareness, mockery, even, of the patent vulnerability she had revealed at his kiss, but the hard male face was set in business mode and the deep voice was brisk and even. The cold, commanding, high-flying tycoon was back in full regalia, the fascinatingly sensual dinner companion a distant memory as she faced him across the breakfast table.

'Good morning.' She was aware that her colour was high, and as the waiter hovered for her order she concentrated on the menu and regained her composure before glancing at him again. It was the lowering of that newspaper that had done it, sent her body into an abrupt awareness of him as she had met the piercing silver-grey gaze so suddenly.

'I'm afraid I've already eaten.' He gestured to the plate that the waiter was just removing before ordering more coffee, his voice pleasant and natural. 'But perhaps we could share a pot of coffee before I dash off? I've a business appointment at nine at the other end of the city and they're sending a helicopter shortly.'

'Are they?' How the other half live, she thought silently. Travelling by helicopter to a business appointment clearly meant as little to him as catching the number fourteen bus to Piccadilly. 'I hope your meeting goes well,' she added politely as her senses registered the jet-black hair slicked back and gleaming with health, the harsh, rugged features that were far more attractive than any pretty-boy good looks.

'So do I.' He grimaced as he folded the newspaper before settling back in his chair in a way that indicated his ease with himself and the world about him. 'But it won't be very pleasant, at least not initially.

'I have the distinct impression I'm being backed into a corner by certain individuals and I don't like that, I don't like that at all, so it will have to be the tough-guy approach, with all guns firing. All's fair in love and war, but I won't allow myself or the company to be manipulated by anyone, and they might as well realise that straight off.'

She couldn't imagine how anyone would have the nerve to take such a liberty, ever, but she merely nodded a response as the waiter returned with a pot of steaming coffee.

'Are you satisfied with the way things are panning out, Josie?'

'What?' For a stunningly heart-stopping moment she thought he was referring to the night before, before common sense reasserted itself just in time for her to avoid making a complete fool of herself.

'Yes, I think so,' she said quickly, reaching for the cup of coffee he had just poured for her with a smile of thanks. 'Certainly all the main groundwork is straight in my mind, although I may need to liaise with someone in the know fairly frequently over the next few weeks. The fact that you are having the launch in your own grounds helps, of course, although caterers and suchlike tend to be booked months and months in advance these days. Have you a final completion date on the yacht yet?'

'The end of August.' He shook his head slowly. 'It's a little tight but it can't be helped; it will still give us a couple of months to play around with. Mike assures me that's more than enough time.'

Does he? Josie thought grimly. Well, it wasn't Mike who had the responsibility for pulling all the threads together on this one, was it? Mike, unfortunately, had a way of promising the moon at times to prospective clients, in an effort to get their business, and it didn't always bode well for his employees, who were left to pick up the pieces when something in an impossibly tight schedule went wrong.

'I wouldn't put it quite like that,' Josie said carefully. 'There is a great deal to organise and arrange, and the time-table will be a narrow one—'

'You aren't telling me you can't cope with it, are you?' Luke asked coolly.

'No, I'm not saying that.' Josie took a deep breath and forced a polite smile to her face. 'I'm just explaining that we have a great deal of work to do and very little time to do it.' She resented the way he had immediately assumed she couldn't handle the project, but knew she would get nowhere by letting her indignation show. 'But that is what you have employed me to sort out,' she added, with studied control.

'And you feel confident about the project?' He took a long swallow of black coffee. 'That you can please me?'

She eyed him for a moment before she spoke. With anyone else but him—anyone—she would have taken that question purely at face value, but there had been an in-flexion in the deep, silky voice she was sure she hadn't imagined. But then his gaze fixed on her again and his face was quite expressionless.

She had to stop imagining things around this man, she told herself firmly; she really did. 'Of course. I wouldn't have accepted the job otherwise,' she replied with careful formality.

'No, silly of me to ask.' The silver eyes narrowed suddenly, but gave no indication of what he was thinking. 'Do you like boats?' he asked quietly.

'I haven't had much to do with any.' She forced a bright smile. 'Only a little rowing boat when I was younger, which wasn't quite in the same league as the Hawkton cruisers!'

'Oh, yes?' He straightened slightly in his seat, his voice interested but casual. 'And whose was that?'

She blinked slightly, suddenly aware that she didn't want to continue the conversation but unable to think of a way to deflect him from this trip into her past. 'My father's,' she said carefully. 'He was a great fishing enthusiast, and as I shared the bug we used to fish most weekends.' She looked down into her cup as she spoke, her body language making it clear the conversation was at an end, but he failed to take the hint.

'Was?' he asked gently.

'He died thirteen years ago.' She didn't glance up as she spoke, her long lashes shading her eyes from his gaze.

'I'm sorry.' There was a moment's pause and then he spoke again, his voice soft. 'That must have been a difficult time for you.' You'll never know, she thought bitterly. 'And your mother?' he persisted when the silence stretched on.

'She died too, a year or so later.' In spite of all her efforts she was unable to keep her voice completely even, a slight throb that spoke of pain causing Luke's eyes to narrow still further into slits of silver light.

'Any brothers or sisters?'

'I was an only child,' she said flatly. 'As were my parents, which had made the Owens clan a very small one.'

'That's a shame. I approve of big families myself.' His voice sounded as though he was smiling but she didn't raise her gaze to his to find out. He was trying to be pleasant, she knew that, but she could do without it. He always seemed to manage to hit her on the raw. 'I always think the rough and tumble of family life knocks off the rough edges, don't you?'

'No.' The one word was abrupt, bordering on rudeness, and very final. 'Do you want me to fax the final calculations for the day's entertainment and the ball to you here when I've completed them?' Josie asked flatly as she raised her face to his. 'They will be accurate to within five per cent of the total figure.'

'That won't be necessary.' As the waiter arrived with Josie's toast and preserves Luke stood up; his voice was curt. 'I shall be back in England in a few days; they'll do then. Thank you for your help on this, Josie; I look forward to seeing you in the future.'

He left even as her goodbye still hovered on her lips, and as she watched him stride out of the restaurant she felt the strangest desire to call him back, before she rebuked herself sharply for such a dangerous weakness. She was doing some promotional work for him. That was all. *That was all*.

* * *

Back in England, she continued to talk logic and sense to herself all week, and the fact that she was immersed in the *Night Hawk* project helped enormously. She was exhausted by the time she flopped into bed each night but she didn't mind the twelve- to fourteen-hour days that the project warranted. She knew the chaos would die down after the first ten days or so, when all the main points were under control, allowing the theme to emerge.

The first two weeks and last two weeks of a project this size were always the worst; the rest of the time was usually very enjoyable, and she relished seeing a hundred and one threads come together to form a perfect whole. Or what she hoped would be a perfect whole in this case, she thought wryly on the Friday lunchtime as she sat with Penny and some of the other office staff in a small wine bar just round the corner from the office block, sipping mineral water.

'Josie, darling, how are you, sweetie?'

She turned with a smile to meet Charlotte's gushing greeting, although for once she wasn't ready for their usual cut-and-thrust banter.

'Now, correct me if I'm wrong, but a little birdie has told me you've really hit the big time with this last scoop of yours,' Charlotte continued lazily, her hard, light blue eyes anything but.

'Meaning?' Josie decided to play safe and let Charlotte spell it out.

'The Hawkton contract.' The words obviously stuck in the other woman's slender throat. 'I recognised him instantly last week, of course, but he clearly had eyes for no one but you.'

'It wasn't quite like that.' Be pleasant, Josie, she warned herself silently, aware of several pairs of interested ears flapping about her. 'He had narrowed a few firms down to a short list and was doing a little checking-up procedure of his own, that was all. He wanted to see how I worked.'

'Oh, how you *worked* . . .' Charlotte laughed throatily. 'Silly me, and here I was thinking— Well, it doesn't matter what I was thinking, does it? Well done anyway, darling— but just a little word to the wise . . . The man in question can be lethal when work's finished—know what I mean?'

'Not really, but I'm sure you're dying to tell me.' Josie forced a light smile that was the best piece of acting she had ever done.

'The women, darling, the women!' Charlotte waved an elegant hand on which several rings glittered and flashed. 'They just adore him, and if half the rumours are true he adores them right back. Mind you, given half the chance, who wouldn't? He really sets the juices going with that dark, ruthless technique. I've always been a pushover for the "me Tarzan, you Jane" approach, but there just aren't too many men who can carry it off these days,' she finished with a dramatic sigh.

'You're just a pushover anyway, Charlotte.' Her companion, a slender, fair-skinned man in his thirties, obviously didn't appreciate his colleague's comments. 'If half the rumours are true, of course,' he added sweetly, parroting her earlier words with an innocent smile.

'Now, now, darling, keep those sharp little claws under control.' As Charlotte tapped him lightly on the arm with red-tipped fingers she waved a languid hand at Josie. 'See you later, sweetie, and don't forget, he really is the original love-them-and-leave-them type wolf. Not your cup of tea, I'm afraid.'

'Charlotte, I work for him, that's all,' Josie said evenly. 'And you know it.'

'Yes, in your case I probably do,' the other woman acknowledged with a wry smile. 'You really do have the most marvellous control over your libido, darling—'

'Unlike you,' her companion cut in again. 'Which is probably exactly why the man in question had the sense to choose Josie.'

'Sweetie, you really are in the most foul mood...'

As Charlotte and her associate walked off, bickering amiably, Josie caught Penny's indignant glance across the table.

'That woman really is a first-class bitch,' Penny stated flatly. 'Hasn't she heard of losing gracefully?'

'Don't let it bother you.' Josie smiled at her assistant's fierce face. 'That's just Charlotte's way; it doesn't mean anything.' Her casual answer, combined with an unconcerned smile, seemed to diffuse the interest of the other office staff, but as the conversation ebbed and flowed about her Josie's mind was in a different dimension altogether.

So he liked women, did he? Well, so what? She hadn't exactly imagined he was inclined any other way, so it was no big deal to find out he was something of a philanderer. She had seen the way the women hadn't been able to keep their eyes off him in Germany, and what man, when offered it on a plate, would refuse?

He was very attractive, very wealthy and powerful, with an air of dark ruthlessness that could well work as a dangerous aphrodisiac to most females, as Charlotte had pointed out. No. She *hadn't* expected anything different. So why, in view of all that, was it smarting so much? she asked herself with a touch of surprise. And why did she have this ridiculous feeling that the day had just become overcast, grey?

'Are you OK, Josie?' As Penny touched her arm, her good-natured face concerned, Josie was jerked abruptly out of her thoughts to the realisation that she had been sitting in silence for a good five minutes. This wouldn't do; it wouldn't do at all, she thought irritably. If anyone should even begin to guess at what she had been thinking...

'I'm fine, apart from exhaustion and an imminent nervous breakdown,' she joked quickly, forcing a bright smile to her face. 'Thank goodness the main bulk of the decisions have been made now; I can start a normal working routine again until the middle of October. I think I could fall asleep at any time of the night or day at the moment.'

'I don't know how you do it,' Penny said quietly. 'You work far harder than any of the others. Still, it's paid off, hasn't it?'

'Uh-huh.' Josie nodded her agreement as the little voice in her head made itself known again. Yes, her one hundred per cent commitment to her career had paid off, if you could count going home to an empty flat with just Mog for company each night payment, that was. The thought shocked her, coming as it did from nowhere, and she found herself staying even later than usual at the office that evening, simply to prove she was where she wanted to be.

She was just leaving at a few minutes past nine, her briefcase and portfolio full of sketches and papers weighing a ton, when the telephone began to ring shrilly as she reached the far door. She turned, hesitated for a few moments as she waited for the caller to give up, and when it still continued hurried back quickly, expecting it to stop just as she picked it up. It had been that sort of day after all.

'Hello? Top Promotions,' she stated breathlessly as she lifted the receiver to her ear.

'Why aren't you at home with your feline friend?' The dark voice was deep and husky and unmistakably Luke's.

'I— How did you know it was me?' she asked weakly as a little shiver snaked down her spine.

'I could ask you the same thing,' he drawled slowly. 'But to answer your question, what other female would still be working at gone nine on a Friday night? Anyway, I already phoned your flat and there was no reply.'

'I could have been out,' she answered quickly as the shiver was replaced by anger at the fact that he assumed she had nowhere else to go other than home or the office.

'You were. You were at work,' he said calmly. 'And don't get on your high horse, Miss Owens. It was you yourself who told me that the moggy and work filled your days and nights.'

'I did not.' She hadn't, had she? she asked herself helplessly. No, she hadn't. 'I said I had friends and—'

'Why so defensive anyway?' he asked, with a calm arrogance that made her literally grit her teeth. 'There's nothing wrong with working late, especially when the work in question is for me. I find it highly commendable.'

'Do you?' Count to ten, Josie, count to ten, she told herself tightly, the dry, mordant mockery in the deep voice grating on her nerves like barbed wire. The man was impossible! Totally, absolutely impossible—but she wouldn't win in an argument with him; that much she had learnt in their short acquaintance. She took a long, hard breath and forced her voice into tones of honeyed sweetness. 'Then that makes all the long hours worthwhile, doesn't it?' she said, with an innocent sarcasm that wasn't lost on the man listening to her.

'Quite so.' There was a moment of silence and then he spoke again. 'I wondered if you'd like to have dinner tomorrow night and we can discuss how things are going? There are a couple of small points I feel need attention, but I only arrived back in England tonight so I haven't been able to give them my full consideration.'

'Dinner?' Just for a moment, in spite of all her good intentions, and the logical if painful reasoning of the last few days, she was tempted, and that fact alone put steel in her voice. 'I'm sorry, Luke, I'm afraid that's not possible. However, I'd be glad to call in at your office first thing Monday morning, if you like. Would that be soon enough?'

'No problem,' he agreed easily. Too easily, she thought testily. No doubt there were women lining up to have dinner with Luke Hawkton. 'Make it first thing, would you? The day is bound to be chaotic with my having been away for a week.'

'Certainly. Nine OK?' she asked briskly.

'Fine. Allow an hour or two, would you?' he said coolly. 'It might take us some time to come to that mutually agreeable solution you mentioned once before. Now,' he continued before she had a chance to speak, 'I'd call it a day if I were you and go home and feed that poor animal of yours. What's it called, by the way?'

'*It* is a he, and Mog is not a "poor animal",' she said tightly, unable to keep the note of indignation out of her voice. 'He has a wonderful life.'

'I've no doubt about that. If I lived with you I'd consider myself a very fortunate animal too,' he said solemnly, but she had caught the thread of amusement in his voice and found herself smiling in return even as she kept her voice cool and distant.

'I'm sure you would. Goodnight, then.'

'Goodnight, Josie. Sweet dreams,' he said softly, that husky note in his voice more pronounced.

Sweet dreams, indeed! She stood staring at the telephone for some minutes after she had replaced the receiver. How could he make two fairly innocuous words sound so suggestive? she asked herself weakly. Or was it her imagination playing tricks again?

'Home, Josie.' Her voice echoed round the empty office and she shook her head as she retraced her steps to the door. Talking to herself now? That was all she needed!

As the lift carried her swiftly downwards she glanced at her watch with a little frown. Half past nine. Mog would be starving by now. Her flat was on the second floor of a beautifully converted house in Chelsea, and the fact that the property boasted a long narrow walled garden and that the caretaker, who had his own basement flat, had two amiable tabby cats of his own had made having Mog no problem.

He came and went pretty much to his liking, both her own front door and the back door having catflaps, and old Mr Jones was always happy to feed him if she was away. But Mog was a cat with very definite ideas of his own, and a late evening meal would be met with cold, green-eyed disapproval and a rigidly stiff tail.

She answered the security guard's cheerful goodnight without really thinking about it, her mind occupied with getting home as quickly as possible. The tube was the obvious solution but she didn't really like travelling on her own late in the evening; there had been one or two occasions recently when she had felt uneasy. She could get a bus but at this time of night they were notoriously unreliable...

No, she'd get a taxi if she could find one, she decided as the massive plate-glass doors of the office building slid open and she emerged, briefcase over one arm and both hands clutching the bulging portfolio, into the warm London night.

'You look as if you could do with a lift.'

She froze for just one moment as the deep, husky voice halted her in her tracks, before turning slowly and surveying the beautiful dark blue Mercedes parked regally on double yellow lines a foot or so away.

'How—?'

'I phoned from the car.' He anticipated her question before she could voice it. 'Do you often wander about

London late at night on your own?' he added, with definite condemnation.

'I would hardly term hailing a taxi as wandering,' she said crisply as she remained standing where she was.

'Well, I damn well would—'

'And half past nine on a June evening can hardly be considered late,' she interrupted icily. 'I can't see—'

'Why didn't you call a taxi from the office?' he asked with equal frostiness. 'Or is that too obvious a thing to do?'

'Now look here, Luke Hawkton, how I travel to and from work is absolutely nothing to do with you,' she said angrily as the last of her precarious control melted under her quick temper. 'I've managed perfectly well for the last ten years, so I don't think I need any lessons in safety now.'

'I do.' He glared at her as he left the car in one swift movement to stand before her, big and dark and undeniably menacing. 'And for crying out loud stop being so damn ridiculous and get in the car. You know as well as I do how the crime rate has gone haywire in the last few years, and a tiny little thing like you, struggling along with a bulging briefcase—a *tantalisingly* bulging briefcase, I might add, to someone living rough on the streets—is just asking for trouble.

'It was only a couple of weeks ago that a woman was mugged, raped and left for dead in an alley just a block or so from here, and she was a darn sight bigger and heavier than you. *And* that incident happened at six o'clock on a Monday evening in the rush hour. So don't talk to me about safety, Josie.'

She stared into his dark countenance angrily, opened her mouth to argue the point further, and then her courage evaporated suddenly at the furious expression on his face. He was angry. He was *really* angry, she thought in surprise. The black eyebrows were frowning over eyes that had turned a stony cold grey and his mouth was a grim line in the tautness of his face.

Why was he so angry? Because she had defied him? Or because he cared that she might get hurt? she asked herself weakly. She suddenly felt it was more likely the latter than the former, and the thought turned her meekly in the direction of the car. She walked past him and seated herself in the passenger seat without saying a word. He stood for one more moment on the pavement before swinging round himself and sliding into the car, banging the door with unnecessary force.

He started the car without speaking, his profile cold and taut, and as she glanced round she noticed a suitcase slung on the back seat and a large black briefcase standing on the floor. 'Haven't you been home yet?' she asked in surprise.

'No.' The one word was abrupt and final.

'Oh...' She gazed out of the window as the powerful car drew away, her senses alive to the delicious smell and sheer presence that vibrated from the big male body next to her in the close confines of the Mercedes. 'Thank you for the lift,' she said lamely, after a few tense minutes had ticked by. 'It was very good of you to call by on the off chance.'

'It was on my way home,' he said expressionlessly, his eyes on the traffic.

'Where do you live?' She kept her voice light and even. He clearly hadn't forgiven her yet.

'Greenwich.' He glanced swiftly at her before returning his gaze to the road ahead. 'And don't look so nervous; I'm not going to eat you. I can actually be quite civilised when I try, you know.'

'I'm sure you can.' And he would be a wonderful lover...

The thought was there in the front of her mind before she could push it away, stark and unwelcome and abrupt, and she realised it had been simmering in her subconscious since Germany. It was the word 'civilised' that had brought it to the surface again.

Because he would be deliciously *un*civilised in the throes of passion, she thought helplessly. She knew it. She felt it in her bones. That cool, controlled exterior would melt into a hot sensuality that would take the woman in his arms to the heights... *Stop it Josie*. She shut her eyes tightly for a second in an attempt to block out her thoughts.

But there was something about him, a dark, brooding kind of masculinity, that drew her mind to the physical in spite of herself, and she found it all the more difficult to cope with because nothing of that kind had ever bothered her before. But with Luke Hawkton... She just couldn't ignore it, she conceded helplessly.

'I know you live in Chelsea, but a few directions would be useful.' The deep voice cut into her tortured thoughts, and when she glanced out of the window she realised she was nearly home, the Mercedes having eaten up the miles with consummate ease.

'Of course. Sorry, I was daydreaming,' she said hastily.

'That does my ego the world of good, Josie, thank you,' he said with cool sarcasm. 'Now, the address is Chiltern Close, isn't it? And that's somewhere off Jade Road?'

'Yes. You turn right in a few minutes—I'll tell you when—and then the next street after the traffic lights is Jade Road,' she said as evenly as she could. 'Chiltern Close is the third on the left.'

The Mercedes nosed into Chiltern Close a few minutes later and came to a smooth stop under a large silver birch tree, a line of which bordered the quiet, pleasant road. Oh, help, they were here now, Josie thought desperately, and her mind struggled with the problem that had been occupying her thoughts for the last few moments. He had just flown back from Germany after what had probably been quite a gruelling business trip and he hadn't even touched base yet. She couldn't let him drive away without offering him a cup of coffee and a sandwich... could she?

No, she couldn't; of course she couldn't, she told herself quickly. It would be the height of rudeness, but— She took a deep breath before she spoke. Every instinct in her body was telling her to do just that.

'Would you like a coffee?' She was amazed at how light the words sounded when she felt anything but. 'Or perhaps you want to get straight home—'

'A coffee would be great.' That's your opinion, she thought darkly as she smiled brightly and climbed out of the car. 'Here, let me take those.'

He relieved her of her briefcase and portfolio in one easy movement and then followed her the one or two steps to the front door, glancing up at the large, three-storeyed house as he did so. 'How many flats are there?' he asked quietly as she opened the door into the wide hall, her fingers fumbling with the key and almost dropping it in her agitation.

'Four—one on each floor, including the basement,' she said as she shut the door behind him. 'Mr Jones, the caretaker, lives in the basement flat, and he sees to the other two houses either side as well. The same property company owns them all.'

'Which property company is that?' he asked as he followed her up the narrow stairs leading from the hall.

'Pears.' She was acutely conscious of the bulk of him just behind her, but when she reached the smartly painted door of her flat she steeled herself to open it smoothly this time, and as it swung open Mog was there in front of her, with a mournful and very reproachful long-drawn-out miaow.

'So this is the man in your life?' Luke asked softly as he deposited the briefcase and portfolio on a nearby chair and bent down to stroke the cat, who had totally ignored Josie and now arched ingratiatingly against his legs. 'Yes, I can see why he would be; he's very handsome.'

'You like cats?' Josie asked in surprise. Somehow she hadn't put him down as an animal-lover.

'That doesn't fit your mental picture of me?' Luke asked silkily, the smoothness of his voice at odds with the narrowing of the piercing silver eyes. 'Well, I'm sorry to disappoint you, Josie, but yes, I like cats—dogs too, as it happens.' He straightened, but Mog continued to wind round his legs as his chest rumbled with a loud purr. 'I have several cats at my home in the South of France, and also here in Greenwich, which are ably cared for by my resident housekeepers.'

'No dogs?' she asked carefully, ignoring the first part of the conversation.

'Not yet.' He continued to look at her, his hard face cool and remote and his voice soft. 'They'll wait until I settle down and enter the next stage of my life.'

'Which is?' she asked flatly.

'Family man and attentive husband,' he answered with a mocking smile. 'And I bet you can't imagine that either.'

'No, not really.' She turned away as she spoke, a shaft of pain stabbing at her throat. So he wanted to settle down soon and raise a family? Well, of course he would; she shouldn't have expected anything else. Even the most dyed-in-the-wool philanderer succumbed to the natural human desire to build a nest and raise fledglings eventually. The desire to procreate, to have sons and daughters, was strong in any man, but especially in one as virile and sensual as Luke; it was perfectly normal. Absolutely to be expected.

She walked through to the kitchen, her back rigid.

'Josie?' His voice caught at her, and there was a note in it she didn't understand but didn't dare try to explore. 'What's wrong?'

'Wrong?'

She bent to the low cupboard that housed Mog's cat food and took a long, deep breath before reaching for a tin and turning to face him. He was standing in the kitchen doorway and she noticed suddenly that he looked tired, that there were dark shadows under his eyes which brought the prominent cheekbones forward and gave the grey eyes an even more silvery hue. And the feeling that it aroused in her was as unwelcome as it was unexpected. She didn't want to feel tenderly towards him; she didn't dare.

'Nothing's wrong,' she said carefully. 'What ever gave you that idea? It's just that Mog has ignored me since I walked through the door and that tells me His Highness is displeased that his dinner's late.'

'Right...' He grinned at her, and she didn't like what that did to her fragile equilibrium either. 'A demanding male, is he?'

'And how.' She was relieved the mood had lightened, but as she made the coffee she found she was still all fingers and thumbs, and her agitation wasn't helped by the fact that Luke was standing there leaning against the kitchen door with his hands in his pockets, watching her as she worked.

'Would you like something to eat?' she asked expressionlessly as the coffee-machine began to bubble and splutter. 'I usually shop at weekends, so there isn't much in, I'm afraid, but I could rustle up a few ham and salad sandwiches, or an omelette if you'd prefer?'

'A round of sandwiches would be welcome.' He gestured to his tie and jacket. 'Do you mind if I make myself comfortable? It's pretty warm in here and I've only averaged three or four hours' sleep a night over the last week. I don't want to fall asleep on you.'

'Feel free.' She forced a bright smile as her breath stuck in her throat. How had all this come about anyway? If anyone had told her this morning that Luke Hawkton would be disrobing in her flat that night she would have laughed in their face. Suddenly events were galloping away with her and it was too dangerous. *He* was too dangerous. 'Difficult week, was it?' she asked evenly.

'Damn awful.'

He had taken off his jacket and tie, and now, as he undid the first few buttons of his shirt, she really had problems with her breathing. He was too attractive for his own good, or certainly for *her* good, she thought ruefully as she turned determinedly away, taking a few deep, hidden breaths and busying herself with the food. Mog had disappeared through the catflap after his meal for an evening sojourn.

'But everything turned out all right?' she asked after a few moments, when she could trust her voice not to betray her.

'Of course.' There was a touch of arrogance in his voice now. 'I always get what I want in the end.'

'Always?' She nerved herself to turn and face him again as she placed two plates of sandwiches on a tray.

'Always.' He smiled at her, a faintly sensual quirk to his mouth, and she couldn't tell if he was serious or not.

'Lucky old you,' she said lightly as she poured two cups of coffee and placed sugar and milk on the tray.

'Here, I'll carry it through.' He reached over and took the tray out of her hands, the hardness of his thighs as he brushed against her causing a shiver of feeling right down to her toes. 'Lethal' was the word Charlotte had used to describe him and she hadn't been wrong, she thought faintly. More was the pity.

'Nice room.' After he had placed the tray on the low coffee-table he straightened and glanced round the lounge. 'Very nice,' he drawled approvingly.

'I like it.' Her parents' estate had meant she had had no financial problems even before she had secured her highly paid post at Top Promotions, and, knowing that her flat would probably be home for the rest of her working life, she had spared no expense in furnishing it exactly as she liked.

The lounge was a mixture of browns and reds, the full-length dark scarlet curtains that draped the balcony windows rich and warm, complementing the lighter oatmeal carpet and walls, and the big soft suite, in shades of muted red and brown, toning with the whole perfectly. Any wood was a dark, rich mahogany that gleamed and shone, reflecting the bowls of fresh flowers she always like to have around and which filled the flat with the scents of summer.

'Do sit down. You must be starving,' she said, with a prim politeness that spoke volumes to the big, dark man watching her so closely, especially when, having handed him his coffee and sandwiches, she ignored the space next to him on the sofa in front of the coffee-table and perched herself on the very edge of a chair.

'You obviously take a great deal of pleasure in your home,' he said quietly, after demolishing a sandwich in a couple of bites, his gaze lingering on a painting on the far wall. 'That's a Goudge, isn't it?' he asked softly as he turned back to her.

'Yes, it is.' She tried to hide her surprise, which hadn't been very well received when he'd unexpectedly revealed that he liked cats. Tim Goudge had only just arrived on the London scene, and although he was an excellent artist and a very pleasant man he was not well known and had no influential patrons to smooth his way. 'You like his work?'

'My aunt does. She's followed his progress over the last few years in his native Ireland and was quite thrilled when he moved to London. I noticed one of his paintings in that art gallery you promoted, by the way. Was that your idea?' he asked intently.

'Yes.' There was something about the sight of him, relaxed and comfortable on her sofa, with his long legs stretched out in front of him and the muscled power of his chest accentuated by the thin shirt, that was bringing out goose-pimples all over her body.

'I thought so. Arnold White is not exactly a philanthropist at the best of times, and I couldn't see him giving a boost to a new artist unless someone had sold him the line that it would be financially advantageous to do so. *Is* that what you did?' he asked suddenly. 'Promised him he would rake in the filthy lucre?'

'More or less.' She wasn't quite sure if he approved or disapproved of her actions, and her tone was slightly defensive. 'Tim Goudge needed a break and Mr White won't lose by it in the long run. Besides which there were enough well-known artists on view that day to carry ten art galleries.'

'Oh, I'm not criticising your kindness, Josie. Far from it.' He eyed her lazily. 'But it doesn't quite fit in with the hard, formidable career woman image, does it, to go out on something of a limb when there's nothing in it for yourself? You know as well as I do that succeeding in one's native Ireland is quite different from making it in this jungle.'

'I—' How could she answer that? And why *should* she anyway? she thought militantly. She didn't have to explain her actions, good or bad, to him. 'Well, there you go.' She gave him a bright smile that didn't reach her eyes. 'One of life's little mysteries, Luke. Just when we think we've got it all taped we find out how wrong we can be. It happens all the time.'

'Not to me, it doesn't.' He held her glance for one more moment, his eyes piercingly steady, before holding out his cup with an easy smile. 'I'd love one more cup before I go on my way...'

'Of course.' She almost flew out to the kitchen, her thoughts racing. Why should it matter to him what she was really like? He was attracted to her, that much was obvious, but surely the light affairs he indulged in didn't necessitate a baring of the soul? Just the opposite, she would have thought.

'So, dinner's out tomorrow?' She jumped visibly at his deep, husky voice sounded just behind her, and spilt most of the coffee over the worktop. 'How about Sunday?' he asked softly.

'No. No, I'm sorry—'

'Are you?' He had moved to stand just behind her as she busied herself mopping the spilt coffee, her hand shaking. 'You have the most wonderful hair,' he said huskily, his hand moving up under the mass of burnished red curls and stroking her neck in a warm, intimate movement that shocked her beyond measure. 'Like fire, flickering and glowing...

'Why won't you have dinner with me, Josie?' he asked abruptly, and his hand tightened on her shoulder, moving her round to face him. 'Why are you so afraid of men?'

'I'm not!' she said, trembling, her heart pounding so hard it actually hurt. 'That's ridiculous.'

'I don't believe you.' His hand moved to tilt her chin upwards as he stared down into the green-flecked eyes he had been seeing in his dreams for the last week. 'And I don't believe I've been reduced to envying a cat either,' he said broodingly. 'And a ginger tom, at that.'

'He isn't ginger,' she protested faintly. 'He's brindle—'

He bent and took her parted lips in one swift movement, but instead of the fierceness she had expected the kiss was warm and intoxicatingly, wickedly intimate, blanketing her tremulous fears and causing her to shiver in anticipation as it deepened.

She knew she ought to be fighting this, pushing him away, but what her head was telling her was quite ineffective against the pulsing pleasure that had her in its grip as he tasted her slowly, almost leisurely, taking his time about the seduction with an arrogance that was all male.

After a few long, slumberous moments he moved her closer into him, fitting her tiny, slender shape against the swiftly rising desire of his body as he tangled his fingers in the richness of her hair, drawing her head back in order to achieve greater penetration of her mouth. His tongue was hard and thrusting, and she couldn't believe what it did to the sensitised contours of her mouth, but it wasn't enough. She wanted more, much more...

As his hands moved in a thorough exploration of her soft shape, moulding her against his hardness while his lips trailed fire over her skin, she suddenly became aware of her state of undress and exactly how far things had gone.

'No!' She jerked back so suddenly that his fingers, tangled in her hair, wrenched her head painfully before he could let go. 'I don't want this.' She pulled her blouse together with shaking hands.

'Why?' He didn't try to reach for her again as she backed away from him to stand against the cupboard, her eyes wild. He merely folded his powerful arms as he gazed down at her, his eyes narrowed and his mouth taut. 'Why, Josie? What is it that you're so afraid of? Is it me? You think I'm too big? That I'd hurt you?'

'No!' Her embarrassment had turned her face crimson, the turmoil inside her making her feel faint. Why had she allowed him to make love to her like that? Why?

She knew what he wanted but she didn't have the mentality to be able to walk away from him once the affair finished; she just wasn't made like that. The cauterising pain of her early years had burnt any superficiality right out of her. When she gave her body she would give her heart too; she *knew* that. So why had she let things go this far? He would think she was a tease, the sort of woman who found it fun to excite a man, lead him on, only to draw back at the last moment.

'I'm sorry, I shouldn't have let you...' She shook her head desperately as she ran out of words. 'I'm sorry...'

'I wouldn't hurt you,' he said, with a softness that caught at her throat. 'You have to learn to trust people again, whatever's happened in your past—'

'Leave me alone!' He had to stop, had to cease being so understanding; it was killing her. What would he say if he knew the truth? she asked herself bitterly. That she was damaged, empty, nothing? That her body could do all sorts of things except the one thing it was made for? But then it wouldn't matter for what he wanted her for, would it?

she thought painfully. Sex. A convenient affair. Dress it up how you like, that was what it boiled down to.

Perhaps that incident in the car in Germany had been a softening-up process, a way of convincing her that he wasn't a wham, bam, thank you, ma'am kind of man? That an affair with him would be a discreet, sophisticated kind of liaison? He had said he was past the stage of a sordid back-seat *amour* that night...

'I've told you, I don't want any involvement, Luke, with *anyone*, and I mean it. If you gave me the job thinking I would be in the market to sleep with you—'

'That's enough!' His face was as dark as thunder now, and as she realised what she had just said her hand went to her mouth. 'I'll do us both a favour and forget you said that,' he growled furiously, 'but after we've cleared the air. I don't have to buy my women, Josie, whether it be with jobs or anything else. Is that perfectly clear? *Is it*?' he snarled when she didn't answer.

'Yes,' she whispered through numb lips. 'I didn't mean—'

'I know exactly what you meant, Josie.' He eyed her angrily, his body taut. 'But don't forget the old saying that people who live in glass houses shouldn't throw stones. You respond to me the minute I touch you, and we both know it.' He turned abruptly, walking into the lounge and picking up his jacket and tie from the chair.

'Luke, please let me explain—'

'Explain what? There's nothing to explain,' he said roughly. 'I'll see you on Monday morning.'

He left without looking back, his back straight and his head rigid, and as the front door closed Josie sank down onto the kitchen floor as her legs finally gave way.

How could she have spoken to him like that? She must be mad. He'd never forgive her... And she couldn't blame him. She gazed blankly ahead, her face as white as lint. The way things must be looking to him now she couldn't really blame him at all. Blowing hot and cold wasn't in it...

She groaned softly as she thought of their lovemaking, of what she had invited. But there was no way she could get involved with a man like him, no way at all. However it worked out, it would be a recipe for disaster.

CHAPTER FIVE

THE weekend was an exercise in purging herself of self-pity and regret. She told herself, over and over again, that she had much to be thankful for. Her career was at its highest point ever, she didn't have, and never had had, the financial worries that dogged so many people all their lives, she was young and healthy and strong in mind and body.

And there was even a positive side to the accident too... She would never have to endure plodding about like a hippopotamus with straddled legs and aching back as she had seen so many expectant mothers do. Morning sickness, dirty nappies, broken sleep and all the worries connected with infant inoculations, diseases, illnesses, bullying at school... These would all pass her by.

She was her own person, answerable to no one. She could please herself—travel or stay at home, be up at the crack of dawn or stay in bed all day at weekends... The list was endless. It was the same list she had drawn up thirteen years ago, when she had hauled herself out of the abyss of bitter grief and pain, and it still worked well... mostly.

Monday morning brought a June heatwave that caused the dry London streets to shimmer with light under a cloudless blue sky, and produced a bevy of girls in bright summer dresses and bare legs.

Josie had dressed carefully for the meeting with Luke at nine, her heart pounding like a sledgehammer from the moment she had woken after a restless, troubled sleep and her mouth dry. She glanced at herself in the mirror for the tenth time in as many minutes just before leaving the flat at a few minutes past eight.

The white silk blouse she was wearing was pretty but businesslike, as was the pencil-slim charcoal-grey skirt that reached to just below her calves. She had secured her mass of hair in a high ponytail at the back of her head, as much to allow the air to get to her neck on such a hot day as anything else, and tied it with a white ribbon that hung demurely at either side of the red curls.

The reflection in the mirror bore no resemblance at all to the trembling, distraught figure of Friday night—except for a certain look in the eyes, and a large pair of tinted sunglasses fixed that. She'd do. She nodded to the figure in the glass determinedly. She'd more than do.

She was outside Luke's office at ten to nine, sitting in his secretary's sumptuous outer room, and the sheer force of his wealth and power hit her afresh. The building was huge, and all owned by Hawkton Enterprises, and here on the top floor, where the élite lived and breathed, it was all ankle-deep carpeting, hushed voices, model-girl secretaries and designer suits.

Luke's own secretary looked as though she had just stepped out of a top fashion magazine, every glossy blonde hair in place and her tall, slim figure elegant and perfectly clothed in a close-fitting dress that must have cost a small fortune. 'Mr Hawkton won't be long.' The beautiful face gave a smile in which ice seemed to tinkle. 'He has someone with him at the moment.'

'Thank you.' Josie nodded and then reached for her briefcase, extracting a few papers from within and studying them while she waited, really to give her hands something to do as she fought the inclination to be intimidated.

At exactly nine o'clock the door to his office opened and she heard his voice from within just as the most voluptuous brunette she had seen in a long time sauntered out.

'I'll see you tonight, Catherine. I really can't discuss it any longer this morning. I have an appointment at nine and I shall be tied up all day.' He appeared in the doorway as he finished speaking, glancing across at Josie impatiently. 'Good. You're here. Come through.'

'Bye, then, darling. See you later.' The brunette's voice was a low drawl, the glance she gave Josie dismissive.

Josie switched her mind to automatic as she walked through into Luke's office, but the incident had made her back stiffen with hurt pride and confirmed everything she had thought about the big, dark man in front of her. She had been right not to get involved with him, so right, she thought grimly as she seated herself in the large chair in front of his huge desk. She would have been one tiny notch in his belt, that was all.

'Good morning.' She knew her voice was cold but she didn't care.

'Good morning.' He flung himself down in the massive leather chair with his back to the window, the white sunlight streaming in through the plate glass and turning his face to shadow. 'That was my—'

'Shall we get started?' she interrupted coolly. He needn't spell it out; she knew *exactly* who that female was, and if he thought he was going to rub her nose in it to punish her for her behaviour on Friday night he could forget it. 'I know you're a busy man.'

'Josie—'

'I'm here to do the job you are paying Top Promotions a fortune to do,' she said icily as her stomach clenched in a giant knot. 'And that is the *only* reason I'm here.'

'*For crying out loud, woman*—'

'Do you want to see the plans and figures?' she asked hotly as her control slipped a little. 'I thought it was so urgent I had to be here at the crack of dawn?'

He stared at her for a long moment, muttered something that sounded incredibly rude under his breath, then took in a hard, rasping pull of air through his clenched teeth. 'Fine. If that's the way you want it, fine,' he said tightly. 'What the hell I bothered for in the first place I don't know—'

'No one asked you to bother.' She stared at him, willing the tears that were welling in a hard lump under her breastbone under control. She would not cry in front of him; she would not. 'According to you I got this job on the merit of my work, and I can assure you that I'll give you one hundred per cent effort at all times. I do find it difficult to work miracles at times, whatever Mike says, but I'm trying . . .' She bit down on her lip as she felt her voice shake and couldn't continue.

When he stood up and moved round the desk she tensed, expecting him to touch her, remonstrate with her—something. But he merely walked straight out of the room, leaving her alone as he closed the door firmly behind him.

She sat for long minutes as she brought her emotions and temper under control again, horrified at what she had said and done. He must think she was some sort of nutcase, she thought miserably. Neurotic, unbalanced—

As the door opened again it cut off her thoughts like a dash of icy water and she nerved herself to look up.

'Coffee?' He was carrying a tray, and from the horrified expression on his secretary's face as she carefully shut the door behind him it was a first for him. Multi-millionaires don't often fetch their own coffee, Josie thought on a burst of hysteria that she squashed immediately.

'Yes, thank you.' He had given her a chance to recover, she knew that, and she ought to apologise for her behaviour. She knew that too, but she didn't trust her voice enough yet.

They drank the coffee in silence, and although she was more uncomfortable than she had ever been in her life the hot liquid did help to steady her nerves. 'Luke, I'm sorry. That was very unprofessional,' she said quietly as she placed the empty cup on the tray.

'Forget it.' His voice wasn't unkind but it was distant. 'If you're ready, we'll go through those queries now.'

And that set the tone for the hour she spent with him. He was cool and reserved and very correct, and, although she knew that that was the way it had to be, *needed* to be, for her to continue to work for him, that inconsistent quirk of her emotions that had reared its head more than once where he was concerned had her feeling miserable.

She gathered her papers together just before ten, outwardly calm and inwardly more confused than ever, and once she had packed them away stood up quickly, her face straight.

'Thank you for all your hard work, Josie.' He had stood up too, and now reached across the desk and shook her hand, his grip firm and friendly, nothing more. 'I'm sure it's all going to come together beautifully.'

'I shall make sure it does.' She smiled carefully. 'Goodbye for now.'

'Goodbye.'

She could feel his eyes boring into her back as she crossed the room on legs that mercifully obeyed her, nodding to the secretary in the outer room with a composure that was all feigned before hurrying to the lift in the corridor outside. It was empty, and once she had pushed the button and it had begun to move downwards she leant against the carpeted wall and closed her eyes tightly, biting on her lip painfully.

What on earth had possessed her to react like that to his girlfriend? She had been stupid, so stupid . . . She groaned out loud and pressed her hands to her hot cheeks. Who he saw and when was absolutely nothing to do with her. He was a free agent, as free as a bird. She'd had no right to cause such a scene.

She still couldn't believe she'd behaved like that, she thought dismally, bending down and picking up the briefcase as the lift slid to a halt, and taking a deep breath before she walked into the vast reception area of Hawkton Enterprises. Unprofessional wasn't the word . . .

She continued to feel wretched all that day, but as the week progressed the embarrassment and humiliation faded a little, and she was able to think of the incident without wishing the floor would open and swallow her whole—just.

Friday morning came and went, and by the evening she had acknowledged to herself that he wasn't going to ring her and that she was glad. *Glad*, she repeated fiercely to herself as she rode home by taxi at the sensible time of six-o'clock.

Saturday she spent cleaning the flat from top to bottom, before going out with friends in the evening to an exclusive nightclub where the cost of food and drink was astronomical and the DJ leered at her all night.

Sunday was no better. Owing to the fact that she had been unable to get to sleep until the sun had been well and truly in the sky, she slept till late afternoon, when she awoke with a sickening headache to the sound of someone banging on the door. It was only then that she remembered she had invited a friend round; she had just passed through a particularly messy divorce and had come for an evening of encouragement and commiseration.

She worked hard the next week, throwing herself into the project with a single-mindedness that earnt approval from Mike and Andy and faint awe from Penny. But as usual work proved the therapy she needed. She spoke to Luke twice by telephone over that time and the calls were formal and businesslike; nevertheless the deep, husky voice left her trembling and flushed for a good hour after they had finished.

A blazing hot June gave way to a sultry, humid July, and when, on the second of that month, exactly a month after the first fateful meeting in Mike's office, she received a late afternoon call from Luke suggesting that she fly out to his home in the South of France to familiarise herself with the house and grounds, she found she could answer with only a trace of breathlessness in her voice.

'Yes, I was going to suggest something like that myself within the next week or two. I think we're just about ready for the next stage now, and it would be good to meet the French caterers face to face and iron out every detail there.'

'Right.' Luke's voice was remote, almost expressionless. 'I'll come with you. There are certain points I want to pick up on myself, and it might be useful if I'm there to smooth the way in the preliminaries.'

'There's really no need for that.' She had spoken too sharply and too quickly, and she forced her voice into a lower, smoother pitch as she continued. 'I know how busy you are, and things are well in hand, I promise. The fair is already booked for three days—the day preceding and following the launch as well as the launch day itself—and the ice rink will be constructed at the end of September. I don't think—'

'Be that as it may, I shall feel happier accompanying you.' This time the dark voice left no room for protest. 'If we fly out on the seventh and return a couple of days later will that suit you?'

'Yes.' Her tone said no. 'But I don't feel it's necessary for you to have to put yourself out like this. I'm sure—'

'Josie...' His voice was patient, insultingly so. 'What I like and do not like *is* now your problem, OK? And what I like at the moment is a trip to France on the seventh. So, we go to France on the seventh.'

She held the receiver slightly away from her ear as she stared at it, hard. So he hadn't forgotten the haughty words she had thrown at him at the first meeting weeks ago, she told herself silently. The irony of them had crossed her mind more than once since she had started working for him, but she had hoped, in her naïvety, she acknowledged bitterly, that he had put them out of *his* mind. But she might have known... She glared at the receiver now. That computer he called a mind wouldn't forget or forgive any slight to the great Luke Hawkton, would it? And it was just like him to bring it up now.

'Josie?' The tone was cold. 'Did you hear what I said?'

'Yes, I heard you.' She took a deep breath. She could have counted to ten several times as he waited for her reply, but she still needed another few seconds to bring her voice under perfect control. 'The seventh.'

'My secretary will be in touch with the flight details,' he continued smoothly, 'and I would like you to bring all the necessary paraphernalia regarding the ice rink—we can formalise that too while we're there.'

'Right,' she said flatly, her voice short.

'And don't sulk.' There was that tinge of amusement in his voice which she had recognised more than once in his dealings with her, and which grated unbearably. 'You are a worldly-wise, forceful career woman by your own admission, and such women don't throw tantrums, Josie—or didn't you know?' he added wickedly.

'I wouldn't dream of throwing a tantrum,' she answered immediately, her voice outraged. 'And I *never* sulk.'

'I will take that with an enormous pinch of salt,' he returned drily. 'Goodbye for now.' He had replaced the receiver his end before she could formulate her fury into words, which was probably just as well, she reflected later, after her anger had cooled.

And that annoying trait in her character, honesty, forced her to admit that what he had said was absolutely right too.

Business women of her calibre didn't sulk—it just wasn't done in the marketplace—but somehow with this man all her cool constraint and tight discipline went flying out of the window as soon as he opened his mouth. Why did he get under her skin like this? she asked herself helplessly as she finished the last of the work on her desk and prepared to leave the office. Why, why, why?

'Hear you're taking a trip on the seventh.' Andy popped his head round her door as she clipped the lock on her briefcase shut. 'With Luke Hawkton, to look over the site,' he added meaningfully.

'So it would seem,' she answered a trifle absently as she reached for a big folder, her mind far away with the problem it had been gnawing at for the last hour or so, since Luke's phone call—namely, the man himself. 'How did you know?'

'I was informed by his esteemed secretary,' Andy said a little testily. 'That woman has got a real way with her, hasn't she?' He grimaced disapprovingly as he shook his head.

'You want to meet her in the flesh,' Josie said drily.

'No, funnily enough, I don't.' Andy grinned at her, then his face straightened. 'Just watch your step with him, won't you? That's all. I know he's an old friend of Mike's but that's no recommendation, frankly.'

'Watch my step?' She stared at Andy in amazement. 'What do you mean?'

'You know what I mean,' he said uncomfortably. 'Now, I'm not insinuating anything about your morals, Josie— far from it—but if just a quarter of what is said about the guy is true he's got quite a way with the women, and you know the temptations on these trips. Things can just . . . happen.'

'Nothing, but *nothing* is going to "just happen", Andy, I can assure you,' Josie said firmly, not quite sure whether to be touched by his obvious concern or annoyed at his assumption that she was unable to deal with a pass from the opposite sex. 'I have met quite a few Luke Hawktons in my time.'

'Oh, no, you haven't.' Andy stared at her from under beetling brows. 'You *definitely* haven't, so don't under-estimate the guy, Josie. He's ruthless and hard and quite single-minded when he wants something. There's more than one man who would think twice before tangling with Hawkton Enterprises, I can assure you.'

'You're talking about business,' Josie said quietly. 'That is quite different from how he deals with women, I'm sure.'

'I wish *I* was.' Andy moved across and stood in front of her, his round face troubled. 'Look, Josie, I'm old enough to be your father—nearly your grandfather,' he added wryly, 'and I've known you for a good few years now. You keep yourself to yourself and that's fine, I'm not knocking it, but where someone like Luke Hawkton is concerned...' He scratched his grey head as he searched for the right words. 'Well, I just want you to be aware of the pitfalls.

'I don't know what happened in your life before you came here but I do know that since you've worked for me you haven't spread it around. You haven't had time, for one thing,' he added ruefully. 'You're a first-class employee and I appreciate that—it's rare these days—but I look on you as a friend too and I know that, whatever front you like to put on to the rest of the world, underneath you're as soft as butter. Am I wrong?' he asked abruptly as her face turned scarlet.

'I—' She didn't know what to say; he had taken her completely by surprise. 'Andy—'

'I don't want to see you get hurt, Josie.' Now the velvet brown eyes were definitely concerned. 'You've been on edge ever since you came back from that Germany trip, and it's the first time I've seen you like this. Now, it could just be the enormity of the job, but I don't think so.' He eyed her soberly. 'And I don't intend to pry either.

'Just watch yourself, that's all I'm saying, and I hope you take this in the spirit in which it's meant. I'm only concerned for you, girl. I might be something of a slave-driver, but underneath this gruff exterior beats a heart of pure gold.' He grinned at her as he attempted to finish the conversation on a lighter note.

'Most people would say steel.' She smiled too, although his words had shaken her more than she cared to admit. 'And don't worry, Andy; I haven't reached the great age of twenty-eight without learning how to duck and dive a little.'

'Good.' He patted her on the arm before walking to the door. 'But do me a favour and take a few more boxing lessons before the seventh, OK? Get the ducking and diving technique you mentioned polished, eh?'

Josie stared after him for a long, long time after he had left. Yes, she'd do that. She would be a fool not to.

That conversation was at the forefront of her mind the following Monday morning as she boarded the plane, with Luke big and dark at her side. His chauffeur had arrived for her at the flat earlier that morning before driving on to Hawkton Enterprises, explaining as he did so that an unforseen emergency had detained Mr Hawkton, who sent his apologies. They had reached the airport with minutes to spare, but their path had been smoothed with the oil of power and wealth, which had got them to their seats with consummate ease.

Josie had never travelled business class before, but she was determined not to let it show, accepting the overall luxury and comfort as though she'd been born to it.

'Comfortable?' As she sipped her iced mineral water she nodded primly in answer to Luke's question, permitting herself a cool smile as she did so.

'Very, although you really needn't have got me a seat with you; I'd have been fine in Economy.'

'Are you trying to annoy me, Josie?' The tone was mild, his eyes anything but.

'Of course not.' Her colour had risen but there was nothing to do but ignore it. 'But as your employee I don't expect—'

'I don't know what kind of clowns you usually deal with, but my *employees*—' there was a faint emphasis on the last word '—travel with me or not at all. Got it?' he asked grimly.

'You're very generous.' She managed a tight smile through gritted teeth. 'Would you like to look at the modifications to the sketches for the ice rink?'

'No.' He eyed her darkly. 'I would like to put my head back and sleep. I was in my office until ten last night and back there at five this morning, and the previous week wasn't much better, so if it's all the same to you...?' He adjusted his seat, undid his jacket and loosened his tie then leant back, closing his eyes as he settled his big frame more comfortably.

She waited until her breathing had returned to normal and then dared a look at the relaxed masculine figure at her side. The hard jaw already bore a dark shadow, and just under the cleft in his chin she could see a tiny cut where he had nicked himself shaving. For some reason that little indication of susceptibility, the knowledge that he was as vulnerable as the next human being in certain situations, brought an ache to her lower stomach and a constriction in her breathing that made her hands damp.

She tried to tear her eyes away but found herself surveying him hungrily in spite of herself—the way his thick, short eyelashes brushed the tanned skin, the heaviness of his brows, the web of laughter lines fanning from the corners of his closed eyes. It was a male face, sensual, virile—

'Can I get you anything?' The smooth, cool voice of the stewardess brought her eyes snapping upwards, and she blushed as hotly as if she had been caught doing something indecent, her cheeks burning until they matched the colour of her hair.

'No—no, thank you,' she said hastily as she reached for a magazine at her elbow. 'I'm fine.'

For the rest of the short flight she kept her eyes very firmly on the magazine on her lap, although she didn't take in a word of what she professed to read as she repeated the ground rules she had drummed into herself over and over again in her mind.

This was a business trip, pure and simple. Admittedly she was staying at his house—she hadn't been able to get out of that one, despite two or three phone calls, the last of which had been both abrupt and terse on Luke's side— but that shouldn't be too much of a problem if she remembered she was an employee in his service, nothing more. She was here to work—he had women like that voluptuous brunette, Catherine, for his other activities—and she had no doubt at all that the dark-haired siren would know exactly how to please an experienced man of the world like Luke. Whereas she... She wouldn't have a clue, she admitted silently. Not a clue.

'Here we go. The car should be waiting outside.' As they left the plane Luke took her elbow in a firm grip, and he steered her through the airport formalities, his large bulk protecting her from the carelessly carried suitcases and sharp elbows that her tininess always seemed to bring her into contact with. She was vitally conscious of him at her side, every nerve in her body sensitised and tight as she struggled to maintain her aplomb.

As they stepped through the massive glass doors of the airport terminal the light outside was blinding, a sizzling hot sun blazing down from a sharp, crystal-clear blue sky in which there wasn't the faintest trace of a cloud. The air was dry and scorchingly fierce, the lack of trees and mile upon mile of parked cars creating their own mini furnace.

'It will be better in the car.' Luke had seen her wince as the heat attacked the sensitive pale skin that went with her colouring. 'Have you brought some sunblock?'

'Sunblock?' She stared at him in surprise. She should have done—she always, *always* did when she went abroad—but this time she had forgotten. And it would be *this* time, wouldn't it? she thought balefully, acutely aware of those silver-grey eyes watching her so knowingly. 'I thought I'd get some here,' she lied airily, just as a stunningly beautiful pale gold Rolls-Royce drew up beside them, complete with chauffeur in matching livery.

'On time as always, Louis.' The chauffeur nodded and smiled a greeting before busying himself with the suitcases. Luke glanced down at her lazily. 'The car has an excellent air-conditioning system, so you should be more comfortable inside, and the suncream is no problem. We have a number of creams and oils at the house—a necessity through the summer here. My housekeeper's grandchildren visit several times a week to play in the pool and they are all very fair, so I'm sure there will be something suitable.'

'Oh, right. Thank you.' As she slid into the magnificent car she almost felt like royalty for a moment, before she reminded herself that she was in exactly the same position as the chauffeur in front. She was a paid employee, nothing more, and this seductive style of living—and it *was* seductive, she admitted to herself—was just a brief glimpse of how the other half lived. But she could enjoy it while she had the opportunity, she thought wryly as the big car purred out of the airport. She would probably never get the chance to travel in such luxury again.

Luke's château was situated halfway between St Tropez and Toulon, with its own private stretch of beach and small harbour, and they drove straight there, past grand casinos and luxury hotels and mile upon mile of golden sand fringed by an azure-blue sea, with waving palm trees completing a picture of pure fantasy.

'It's beautiful here,' Josie said quietly as the cool car whisked them through streets in which every other vehicle was a Mercedes or a Ferrari.

'You think so?' Luke smiled down at her, faintly amused by her rapt contemplation of the view beyond the window. 'I guess it has its own type of charm, but the real South of France is inland, and that really is beautiful. I spent a good deal of my childhood exploring the region with John on our bikes—we'd take off for days at a time.

'You wait till you see lavender fields in full bloom, or smell the perfume of mimosa and scented olive groves on a still summer's evening as you sit on a hill overlooking a sleepy medieval village—' He caught her look of astonishment and stopped abruptly, his mouth curving in a sardonic smile. 'We were perfectly ordinary little boys, Josie,' he said softly, 'and we did the camping trips and nights under the stars that all children enjoy.'

'Perfectly ordinary'? she asked herself in disbelief. Did he really believe that? Those 'perfectly ordinary' children had been the sole heirs to a vast empire that provided daily bread and butter for thousands of people. He really couldn't say that was ordinary, could he? And when he'd ridden home after one of those camping trips he had stepped back into a world of wealth and power and servants, where his every need had been taken care of. 'Didn't your parents worry that something might happen to you both?' she asked quietly, careful not to betray her thoughts.

'Not really...' He paused reflectively. 'Well, perhaps my mother on occasion. My father was a very tough individual and he brought John and me up to think and act for ourselves, but my mother was born in Italy to a family of considerable wealth. When she was a little girl one of her brothers was kidnapped by the local mafia and held to ransom; he was returned unharmed once the price for his freedom had been met but I think the incident still haunts her to this day.

'However, she was and is a sensible woman, and she knew she couldn't keep two boys wrapped up in cotton wool. Once she had drilled us in basic road sense and the inevitable "no talking to strangers" she had the sense to let us go. Claude, our gardener's son, who was eight years older than us, used to come with us at first, but once we reached eleven or twelve we used to give him the slip.

'We were little terrors sometimes,' he added softly as he looked back on golden summer days that could never be repeated. 'Real little terrors.'

'Did John look like you?' she asked tentatively, unsure of how much she could ask without raking up painful memories.

'We were identical.' He said nothing more for a full minute as he remained deep in reminiscences of his own, and then suddenly he shook himself out of it, turning to her with a dry smile. 'I bet you find it hard to imagine two of me, don't you?' he said, with a mocking cynicism that told her he had no doubt as to what her opinion of him was. 'But I often think it must be hard for my mother when she looks at me and sees only one of us; she was so proud of her two boys. The Italian in her,' he added indulgently. 'She is a firm believer in families of eight or nine children, but due to complications when she had John and me more children were out of the question.'

'I see.' She forced her voice not to betray the kick in the stomach she had felt at his words. 'So that's where your approval of big families originates, from your mother's genes?' Don't continue this, she told herself silently. Stop now.

'I'm half-Italian,' he agreed easily. The silver eyes had narrowed on her face but she could read nothing in their glittering depths. 'I think four or five children is nice. I'm not quite in the "barefoot and pregnant" league, but my wife will have to produce at least one little male Hawkton to carry on the family name—to satisfy my relations if nothing else. The rest can be girls as far as I'm concerned,' he added magnanimously. 'I like little girls better than little boys on the whole.'

'And big girls too, no doubt.' She didn't know what power was enabling her to sit still and smile as if his words had meant nothing at all, but she blessed it anyway.

'The odd one.' He had become still as he looked at her, the strange hue of his eyes making them seem like piercing lasers. 'The very odd one these days. I find I like them tiny, with hair like tangled red silk and eyes that hold a whole host of shadows I can only guess at—'

'Luke—'

'And here's the château.' They had just approached enormous gates set in a high stone wall through which the car passed smoothly and with a stately flourish that proclaimed it was home. A long, winding drive snaked through bowling-green-smooth lawns dotted with tall, gracious trees and carefully positioned flowerbeds, and beyond the château itself, which was a vision of elegant turrets and domes, Josie caught a glimpse of the turquoise-blue sea, shimmering in the noon-day sun.

'It's something of a fake, I'm afraid,' Luke continued as the powerful car drew up outside the massive studded front door. 'My great-grandfather had it built as a second home just over a hundred years ago in the likeness of an ancient château he admired, but due to the fact that the Hawkton name was only just beginning to establish itself the original building was considerably smaller than what you see now. My grandfather added a complete wing to house the ballroom, and then my father developed the grounds at the back of the house leading down to the sea to include a swimming pool and tennis courts and so on. A French hotch-potch,' he added smilingly.

'Hotch-potch?' Josie stared at him in disbelief before turning to the truly beautiful building of mellow old stone topped by deep red domes and turrets and threaded with tall, narrow windows in which leaded glass glittered and shone. 'You don't mean that,' she said accusingly.

'No, perhaps I don't.' His voice was very deep now, and soft. 'You like it, then?'

'It's exquisite,' she said very definitely.

'Come and see inside.' After he'd helped her from the car she was disconcerted to find that he kept a casual arm round her waist as they walked to the door, which had just been opened by a pretty little maid complete in black dress, white apron and cap.

'*Bonjour, monsieur, bonjour, mademoiselle.*' Bright black eyes flashed interestedly over Josie's face before being demurely lowered as the girl stood aside for them to enter.

'*Bonjour*, Josephine.' As they stepped through the door into a huge sun-splotched hall a large woman in a severe black dress hurried forward, hands outstretched. 'Madame Marat, my housekeeper,' Luke whispered in her ear. 'If you get on the right side of her she'll be a great help to you.'

And if I don't? Josie thought wryly as she smiled and nodded at the somewhat dour-faced Frenchwoman who had clasped one of Luke's large hands in her own plump fingers.

'*Monsieur*, you have been away too long. We have wondered when you would come.' There was no doubting the large woman's pleasure at seeing her employer, and when she was joined by the cook—a thin, angular woman with a tall, bony body who was the very antithesis of Josie's idea of the average cook—she too fairly bubbled with delight.

Well, his staff like him, Josie thought drily as, once the greetings were over, they walked through into a large drawing room. Luke gestured for her to be seated in one of the massive winged armchairs facing the French doors, which were open onto the garden, as he walked across to the drinks cabinet in the far corner of the room. 'What would you like to drink before lunch?' he asked quietly as he turned to face her. 'Sherry, white wine or perhaps a cocktail?'

'Could I have a soft drink, please?' She had decided, after the Germany disaster, that she would never drink alcohol when she was with him again. She needed *all* her mental faculties working and unimpaired, and the fact that she didn't even like the taste of the stuff was an added incentive. And if he thought that was naïve and unsophisticated so be it; she couldn't keep pretending otherwise. 'I don't really like the taste of alcohol,' she added defiantly, in much the same manner as one might throw down a gauntlet.

'No? And you expect me to disapprove of that?' he asked softly, with that intuitiveness she had come to expect.

'I— No, of course not,' she said quickly. 'I was just explaining, that's all.'

'And your rather enthusiastic consumption in Germany?' He had paused with his hand on the cabinet as he held her eyes across the room. 'That was to convince me that you were a seasoned woman of the world, perhaps? A Charlotte Montgomery or someone equivalent?'

'You know Charlotte well?' she asked in surprise, but she chose to ignore the rest of his questions, her heart beating fiercely.

'I don't have to,' he said grimly as he watched the colour stain her pale, creamy skin. 'Charlotte Montgomerys are ten a penny, my deceitful little siren; it is the Josie Owenses that are hard to find and even harder to understand.'

'I—' She searched for something to say, something that would defuse the sudden electricity in the air. 'I just fancied a drink that night, that's all,' she said hastily, her gaze falling away from the directness of his.

'And pigs fly,' he growled darkly. 'Josie, I don't give a damn whether you drink or not, but I do care that you seem determined to present a shallow façade to me at every available opportunity. I don't know the first thing about you, do you know that? You never talk about your family—'

'I told you, I don't have a family any more,' she said tightly. 'I was an only child and both my parents are dead—'

'What about grandparents, old schoolfriends, then?' he asked levelly. 'Who do you spend Christmas with? The New Year?'

'I—' She paused as she fought the panic that was gripping her throat in a stranglehold. When she had left the little village after her mother had died she had said goodbye to everyone who knew her history—apart from one distant old aunt on her mother's side with whom she still corresponded and whom she visited occasionally, simply because the old woman had no other family of her own.

Her own parents had been only children themselves, and both sets of grandparents were long since dead. When she had moved to London it had been a fresh start; it had had to be—she couldn't have coped with anything else. 'I have lots of friends,' she said as calmly as she could, 'but no grandparents or immediate family.'

She raised her eyes and stared at him steadily. 'And I really don't see what it has got to do with you anyway,' she added quietly, praying that the thundering in her ears and rapid beating of her heart weren't obvious to those silver-grey eyes watching her so closely. 'I don't mean to be offensive but it's really none of your business—'

'Perhaps I want to make it my business,' he said softly, his eyes glittering and sharp. 'You intrigue me, Josie Owens. This virginal, don't-touch air is very sexy, do you know that?'

'No.' Her cheeks were burning now but she kept her eyes fixed on his, willing herself not to falter before the rapier-like gaze. 'This virginal, don't-touch air'. What would he do if he knew she *was* in actual fact a virgin? Laugh his head off, no doubt.

'No, I don't think you do, at that.' He looked at her for one more moment before he indicated the cabinet. 'Lemonade, iced orange, lemon and lime . . .?'

'Orange.' Her hands were shaking, she suddenly noticed, and she quickly buried them in her lap, willing the trembling in her body to cease. She was a challenge to him, that was all, and every word Andy had spoken returned in stark red letters in her mind. There was a physical attraction between them and that was *all* it was. The way it affected her was regrettable, but perhaps that was her own fault. If she hadn't shut her emotions away after the accident, refused to let herself get romantically involved with anyone, then perhaps she would be in a better position to put this whole thing into its right perspective.

But because she was who she was she couldn't have done anything else, she argued silently to herself as Luke poured the drinks. She wasn't made for light affairs and the accident had robbed her of the chance to find the sort of man who would want a family, children—the only type of man she could fall in love with, she acknowledged bitterly. Thousands, millions of women the world over might be happy for life with a partner who wanted nothing more than a comfortable lifestyle without the complication of children getting in the way, but without exception she had found that such men did not even stir her to friendship. It wasn't their fault; there was just some essential ingredient missing with them as far as she was concerned.

And she was no use to the other kind. Oh, she had often acknowledged that she might meet someone who would say that it didn't matter, that he still wanted to stay with her even when he knew the truth, but then the relationship would be built on one sacrificing something infinitely precious for the sake of the other, and she couldn't handle inflicting that on someone she loved, seeing a man for whom she cared deeply battling with the demons that had afflicted her simply because he loved her.

And what if, as time went on and they grew older, he grew bitter and disillusioned about the choice he had made? She lived with the knowledge that she could never be a mother because she *had* to; to ask a man to make the same decision about being a father when he was able to have natural children of his own would be too cruel.

'Here.' Her eyes shot upwards from where they had been focused on her clenched hands as she heard Luke's voice, and as he placed the glass of ice-cold orange juice in her hand she saw that his eyes were hooded and remote, unfathomable. 'You are going to drink this and have the excellent lunch Madame Marat has ordered, and later, when we are full and replete, we will doze most of the afternoon away down by the pool under the big umbrellas I bought specially for that purpose. We will swim a little and maybe doze again in the warmth of the evening before wandering back up here to eat an enormous dinner.'

He smiled lazily. 'And you *will* relax, Josie Owens. The world outside, all that has gone before, will not touch you here. I will not allow it, you understand?'

Madame Marat's entrance to call them to lunch saved Josie the necessity of a reply, but as he took her arm and led her through to the magnificent dining room, with its heavy antique furniture gleaming and polished and the walls hung with the sort of paintings Josie knew Mr White would kill for, she knew there was no way she would fall in with his suggestion to laze the afternoon away. It was too dangerous a temptation. Far, far too dangerous. Every instinct, every nerve, every sinew in her body was telling her so.

So. . . she would defy him—again. And she would go on defying him because that was all she could do, her only defence against the treacherous inclination of her heart, which had leapt and raced as he had spoken, frightening her with its longing.

CHAPTER SIX

'OH, HOW lovely.' Contrary to Josie's expectations, they had walked right through the dining room and out onto a massive veranda that ran the length of it, where a small wooden table and chairs were set amidst huge terracotta pots filled with scented shrubs and flowers and trailing ivy. The dining room was situated at the back of the house, and overlooked a large rose garden in which several tiny fountains splashed and shimmered among the velvet blooms of pink and red and white; the air was redolent with their heady perfume and filled with the tinkling sound of water.

'I thought you would prefer a less formal meal,' Luke said softly as he pulled out a chair for her to be seated. 'My mother always takes her meals here when she visits, unless it is an occasion of some sort. My father had the rose garden planted for her some years after they were married. Her parents' home in Italy was built round a large central courtyard which was full of roses, and he felt it would give her pleasure to have a taste of her native land.'

'Was she homesick?' Josie asked tentatively. It hardly seemed fair to question him about his own family and life when she was so reticent in return, but he merely nodded at her, although a shadow passed over his face that she didn't understand.

'Painfully so in the early days, I understand,' he said quietly. 'She came from a large family and they were all very close. She was the first child to leave and found it very hard to adapt. She invited her relations here constantly and gave them far more attention than she gave my father, although she loved him more than life itself. It took her some time to come to terms with what she really wanted, but then something happened and it proved to her that he was more important than anything else in the final analysis. I think their marriage really started from that point,' he added thoughtfully, his eyes looking inwards at something she didn't like to enquire about. 'That's the trouble with love, isn't it?' He suddenly looked straight at her, his eyes intent.

'I don't understand.' She stared at him warily, unsure of how to respond.

'It costs. One way or another it always costs, and there is always one person who sacrifices more than the other.' His eyes were narrowed slits of light and she was unable to read anything in their silver depths. 'Isn't that what you've discovered? This man who's hurt you so badly couldn't have done so if you hadn't let yourself become vulnerable, and that is the most costly thing of all.'

You're on the wrong track, completely the wrong track, she told him silently as she stared back into the harsh, rugged face that was so fiercely attractive. If only that was all it was. But he was right about one thing. Peter had hurt her, devastatingly, savagely so, but not because she had loved him or he her. Nothing as noble as that. And the hurt had been physical and permanent.

She shrugged carefully. 'You've got it all worked out?' she asked flatly. 'Is that what you think? That there has to be some mystery, some heartless lover in my past?'

'No, I haven't got it all worked out, Josie,' he said softly. 'Not yet. But I will.'

'I'm just an ordinary working girl, Luke.' The hard, almost chilling way in which he had spoken frightened her but she was determined not to let it show. That would only add more fuel to the fire. 'I'm sorry to disappoint you, but what you see is what you get. The mystery is all in your own mind.'

'Perhaps.' The silver gaze didn't waver, but as he reached across the table and took one of her small hands in his he turned her fingers over in his hold, exposing her tiny palm and running one finger lightly across it.

'Don't!' She tried to snatch her hand away, but he had anticipated her reaction and the hand holding hers merely tightened its grip.

'I wish I believed it was possible to read what's written here,' he said quietly, his voice deep and husky as his finger continued to wander up and down the softness of her palm until she knew he could feel the trembling he was inducing. 'But perhaps that would be too easy. What do you think?'

'I think Madame Marat is bringing out lunch.' She could have kissed the formidable housekeeper for returning at that precise moment, but Luke shook his head slowly, his eyes tight on her.

'And they say men are unromantic,' he said softly as Madame Marat bustled to their side.

Lunch was light but delicious. The first course, bouillabaisse, a saffron-flavoured fish stew, was presented in small bowls with freshly baked rolls which were still warm from the oven, and the wafer-thin smoked ham and sauté potatoes that Madame Marat served afterwards perfectly complemented the aïoli, a garlicky mayonnaise, and crunchy raw vegetables and salad. The dessert was nothing more elaborate than fresh fruit, but the ripe peaches were huge and juicy and the bowl of succulent dark red cherries temptingly moreish.

'That was lovely.' Josie leant back in her seat as she sipped the last of her sparkling mineral water. 'Does your cook always feed you like that?' she asked lightly, knowing she was deliberately delaying the moment when she informed him that she was going to start work at once.

'Always.' He eyed her smilingly. 'She knows I'm a growing boy.'

'Has she been with you long?' Josie asked curiously.

'For ever.' He shrugged casually. 'She's never married, but Josephine is her niece and the gardener is her brother so it's a small family inside a family. Even Madame Marat was recommended by her ten years ago, when our other housekeeper retired. They used to go to school together, I understand.'

'You place a high value on family, don't you?' she stated flatly.

'I told you, I'm half-Italian.' His face had straightened at her tone. 'It bothers you?' he asked softly, after a few seconds when she didn't speak. 'This family side of things?'

'Good gracious, no.' She forced a light laugh as she stood up, dropping her bleached linen napkin onto the table beside the crystal wineglass. 'It's your business whom you employ; I wouldn't dream—'

'That is not what I meant and you know it.' He too had risen, but his eyes were tolerant as he looked down at her standing so small and slender in front of him.

As she looked up into the darkly attractive face she had a nasty feeling that his indulgence would soon evaporate once he understood she had no intention of falling in with his plans for the afternoon.

'You do not think it is natural for a man to want to settle down with the woman he loves and have children with her?'

The most natural thing in the world, she thought silently as she made her face blank. 'Natural?' She dropped her eyes from the intent silver gaze. Lying was going to be difficult enough, but it would be virtually impossible with those laser-beams dissecting her mind. 'Do you mean to say that if a woman doesn't want children she isn't natural?'

'No, I do not mean to say that,' he said softly as his eyes narrowed faintly. 'And there is no need to protect your career, your...solitary lifestyle so aggressively. I am merely saying that when two people love each other they normally reach a stage in their lives where children become necessary to both of them.'

'In your opinion,' she said flatly.

'Exactly.' His eyes narrowed still more. 'In my albeit humble opinion. I take it high-flying women executives still allow others, even men, to have an opinion?'

'Of course.' There was an aching, painful feeling in her heart region. It was so easy for him, wasn't it? she thought savagely. He assumed, as the vast majority of the population assumed, that when he was ready to procreate it would happen like clockwork. And mostly it did...for other people.

'Well, that, at least, is somewhat reassuring,' he drawled, with a heavy dose of mockery that grated on her raw nerves like a fingernail scratching down a blackboard.

'Well, now I've restored your confidence in the magnanimity of the female race I'll just go and get my briefcase from the hall.' Her voice was cool but her cheeks were flaming as she moved past him and walked swiftly into the dining room. 'I need to get some accurate measurements—'

'Just a moment.' She was halfway across the room when he spoke. Her chin went up, but the tenor of his voice halted her in her tracks and her eyes were veiled and wary when she turned to face him.

'Yes?' She met the lethal glare head-on.

'Your briefcase, along with the rest of your luggage, is now in your room,' he said coldly. 'I will show you where that is so you can change into a swimming costume.'

'I didn't bring one.' It was the easy way out but it was also the truth. She hadn't intended this to be a holiday in even the mildest sense of the word. 'And I really do need to work this afternoon,' she continued carefully. 'I have worked out a very tight schedule—'

'Damn your schedule.' She'd been right; the indulgence hadn't lasted long. 'I've told you what I expect you to do this afternoon.'

For a moment the sheer arrogance in both his voice and stance took her breath away, but then she straightened rigidly, her own eyes flashing sparks and her small chin stuck out at an impossible angle as she faced him. 'Whatever you *expect*, my actual employer is still Top Promotions,' she said stiffly. 'I have never yet wasted company time, and I don't intend to start now.'

'*Wasted?*' If the word had been a gross obscenity he couldn't have reacted more violently.

'Yes, wasted,' she repeated bravely, willing herself not to wilt beneath his rage. 'You said yourself we have to see the caterers and the builders tomorrow, as well as—'

'You don't need to remind me what I said,' he blazed tightly. 'There is nothing wrong with my memory.'

'Well, then...' She took a deep breath and prayed that the intimidation she was experiencing didn't show. 'There are only so many hours in a day—'

'Spare me the platitudes.' He had crossed the room and passed her in three strides. 'Well?' He turned at the door and inclined his head, his eyes icy. 'Are you coming to your room for that damn briefcase or not?'

She'd won? She followed him out into the vast hall and up the long, winding staircase to the first-floor bedrooms with a feeling of disbelief tempering the awe that the beautiful house inspired in her. She had the distinct feeling that very few people had ever won a battle of wills with Luke Hawkton, and she didn't trust him.

'Your room.' He stopped outside a pale oak door halfway down the landing and glanced down at her, his eyes hooded now and distant. 'I'll come back for you in ten minutes, when you've got your stuff together.'

'There's no need,' she said quickly. 'You go down to the pool as you'd planned. I can find my way about and—'

'Ten minutes.' He opened the door and stood aside for her to enter, and after one glance at his set face she scurried inside with a little nod and a muttered 'Thank you'.

Her 'room' turned out to be a suite, with a small sitting room, complete with large desk in one corner, a generous-sized bedroom dominated by a huge four-poster bed, and an extremely luxurious bathroom with every mod con, including a jacuzzi. The colour scheme was one of delicate yellows and soft bluey-greens throughout, the butter-cream walls and high sculptured ceilings adding to the general impression of light and airiness.

'Oh, wow...' She stood for a full minute just gazing about her, totally overwhelmed, before moving to the far wall in the sitting room where three narrow full-length windows allowed the bright sunlight outside to stream into the room. The view beyond was one of rolling lawns and landscaped gardens down to a huge swimming pool some distance from the house, beyond which the lawns stretched again, encompassing three good-sized tennis courts before petering out into snowy white sand and small curling waves as the sea lapped gently up the Hawkton private beach.

'And double, triple wow,' she muttered faintly. Luke had told her, in the details he had sent to the office about the house and grounds, that there were twelve bedrooms in all, and if they were all like this... She shook her head weakly before turning from the window and fetching her briefcase from the desk where it had been placed. 'You're way, way out of your depth, girl.'

She was ready and waiting for Luke's knock, but utterly unprepared for the sight of him as she opened the door. He was naked, almost, a brief pair of midnight-blue swimming trunks his only clothing, leaving his powerfully muscled torso, wide, broad shoulders and sinewy arms and legs bare except for the light covering of dark body hair that curled more thickly on his chest, the tight little corkscrews drawing her eyes in helpless fascination.

He was overwhelmingly, thrustingly, blatantly male, and for a moment the impulse to slam the door shut and run for cover was paramount, before she pulled herself together, dragging her eyes away with an effort as she reached down for the large folder at her feet.

'I'll take the briefcase and portfolio.' His deep voice held a thread of amusement and she knew, she just knew, that he had noticed and planned for her discomfiture. He had a dark blue towelling robe slung casually over one arm that he could quite easily have worn, but it had been a shock tactic, she realised suddenly. He was forcing her to acknowledge the attraction between them.

The thought galvanised her legs in a way nothing else could have done and enabled her to lift her head and give him a hard glare, her eyes focusing directly and only on his face. Out of her depth? Like hell she was, she thought defiantly.

'Thank you,' she said with polite, unsmiling formality.

'My pleasure,' he answered in exactly the same tone.

The rest of the afternoon was an exercise in remaining calm under enemy fire as far as Josie was concerned. He stood by her side, at ease with himself and the world about him, while she measured the proposed site for the fair and the ice rink, the sunlight turning his lean body into shadowed silk and his eyes hidden behind a pair of black sunglasses.

She was painfully aware of every movement he made as he leant over her shoulder to discuss her notes, strolled through the grounds carrying her briefcase and folder from place to place, and led her down to the beach so she could view the small harbour with its jetty and boathouse. His hard, powerful thighs, the way the muscles in his body tensed and relaxed as he moved, the line of hair that narrowed from the thickness on his chest into the brief trunks—she was aware of it all. Every moment. Every *single* moment. And determined not to let him know it.

The anger helped. Anger that she had allowed herself to be put in such a ridiculous position, anger that she had let this man penetrate the barrier she had thought was so strong and firm, anger that he was playing with her, like a satisfied cat with a tiny mouse, and anger that she hadn't won the battle at all. In fact the way she felt was as if the war itself had been well and truly lost. She should have known, when he'd capitulated so easily, that he would have his revenge for her refusal to spend the afternoon in the way he had suggested.

'How much more of the day do you intend to waste?' She had just satisfied herself that the *Night Hawk's* grand entrance would be able to be seen by everyone in the grounds when Luke spoke, his voice calm and unemotional.

'I have not been *wasting* anything,' she said hotly as she swung to face him, a slight breeze from the water's edge where she had wandered blowing a cloud of silky red hair across her face. 'It might have escaped your notice, but I've been working—hard.'

'Nothing you do escapes my attention, Josie.' His mouth twisted in a wry smile. 'Nothing at all. However—' He raised an authoritative hand as she went to interrupt him. 'It is now five o'clock and you have been out here *working*—' he laid a slight emphasis on the last word '—for three hours. Surely even you would concede that a drink by the pool is in order?'

'OK.' Her voice was reluctant, and his eyes narrowed as he watched her.

'But first you change into something more...suitable.' It was an order, not a question.

'I told you, I didn't bring a swimming costume,' she said evenly, blessing the fact.

'That slight oversight is no longer a problem,' he countered smoothly. 'I think you'll find everything you need in your room.'

'My room?' She stared at him, puzzled. 'I don't understand...'

'I asked Josephine to pop into town with Louis and purchase a few things.' His eyes were like weapons, holding hers. 'It would be a crime not to enjoy the pool and the beach while you are here, don't you think?'

'You...' Her voice trailed away as anger replaced blank amazement. 'You did what?' she asked tightly.

'And you needn't thank me now.' He took her arm, ignoring the rage suffusing her delicate features as he began to walk back to the house. 'It is the least I can do for a house-guest.'

'I am not a house-guest.' She shook herself free as the feel of the big, almost naked body next to hers did strange things to her hormones. 'And you know it. I'm—'

'An employee,' he drawled resignedly.

'Exactly.' She stared up at him furiously, tiny and ethereal in the sunlight that turned her hair into living fire. 'What will Josephine and the others think about you buying me clothes like that? It looks as if, as if—'

He cut into her splutterings with a mocking laugh that made her want to hit him—hard. The only problem was that she had a long way to move before she could reach his face. 'It *looks* as if you forgot your bathing wear,' he said with a silky innocence that didn't fool her for a minute. 'Which is what you did, isn't it? Now, stop being so ridiculously narrow-minded. What my staff do or do not think is not your problem; it's mine.'

'I don't believe you,' she spat tightly. 'I just don't believe anyone would resort to such lengths just to get their own way. You've made me look foolish—'

'Not at all,' he said easily, but with a thread of steel now lacing the lazy drawl. 'You do far too good a job of that yourself for me to be able to improve on perfection.' As she raised her hand to strike he caught it easily in his long, capable fingers, shaking his head sorrowfully as he did so.

'Josie Owens, cold, capable career woman, ambitious high-flyer, how could you think of biting the hand that feeds you?' he asked mockingly. 'Hardly the action of a lady with an eye to the main chance.'

'You—'

'But there is fire beneath that cool façade, isn't there?' Suddenly the mockery and cool ridicule had vanished, and his eyes were searching her white face in which two furious spots of colour burnt. 'Fire and a lot, lot more. Who are you really?'

'Now who's being ridiculous?' she asked tightly as she took hold of herself. Losing her temper had been a mistake, a grave mistake, she realised as she looked into the silver-grey eyes that were examining her face. 'I told you before— you are making a mystery where none exists.'

'But you lie, Josie Owens.' He stepped back from her now, folding powerful arms across his chest, and in spite of herself a shiver flickered down her spine in response to the utter maleness of him. 'It's sad but true.'

She disgraced herself further by muttering something very rude that had the black eyebrows rising in sardonic disapproval as he shook his head again, more to annoy her than anything else, she thought waspily. 'Come on,' he said suddenly. 'Enough of this riveting repartee, entertaining though it is. A swim is just what you need.' He took her arm, drawing her into his side as he did so.

It was useless to protest, and she found herself almost carried along by the momentum of his tall, hard body as he whisked her up to the château, not stopping until he had deposited her outside her room. With a deep sigh, he looked down into her breathless face. 'You are going to change into one of the costumes Josephine has so kindly bought for you,' he said expressionlessly, 'and come with me to the pool. If you defy me...' He paused and allowed a twist of his lips that might have passed for a smile if the circumstances had been different. 'I shall come in and undress you myself. OK?'

'You wouldn't dare,' she muttered weakly. 'Not even you.'

'Wrong.' This time the smile was definitely dangerous. 'Quite wrong, my little red-haired sprite, but I won't object if you put me to the test.' He let his eyes run down her slender shape in a mockingly lewd appraisal. 'No, I can promise you that at least,' he said with a lazy thoughtfulness that sent shivers flickering through her again.

She gave him one last glare, opened the door and flounced inside, banging it hard behind her. It was childish but she just couldn't help it, she thought angrily.

She was just preparing to walk over to the horribly expensive-looking bags that took up the whole of the sofa in the small sitting room when a knock sounded on the door, and in the next moment Luke had opened it, amusement etched in every line of his rugged face. 'Yours, I think?' He handed her the briefcase and folder, gave a mocking bow and turned to leave, giving one last parting shot as he did so. 'I will see you at the pool in exactly ten minutes,' he said over his shoulder. 'OK?'

Once he had left, and she was alone, she examined the contents of the bags, which all had exclusive designer names and contents to match. 'He must have spent a fortune,' she mumbled helplessly to herself as she shook out first one, then another, then another beautifully made garment.

There were four bikinis in all, each with matching sarong, shirt and trousers and all quite exquisite. She sat gazing at them for a full minute, her mind racing as she told herself she couldn't possibly accept them, and then she realised with a start of panic that five minutes had elapsed since Luke had left.

She gathered up the nearest bikini—a dainty creation in vivid green silk with soft swirls of mauve and blue—and the corresponding shirt and trousers, and raced into the bedroom, stripping off her clothes and donning the new ones in a fever of fumbling fingers that just wouldn't obey her. She looped her hair into a high knot on the top of her head, glancing at herself in the mirror as she did so and then freezing at the sight of the reflection that stared back at her.

That old saying, 'clothes maketh the man' has a lot going for it, she thought in stunned amazement, or in this case 'maketh the woman'. The loose trousers and open shirt were beautiful and looked as though they had been made for her, deepening the colour of her eyes to a soft, glowing gold in which the flecks of green stood out with a luminescent quality that highlighted her clear, creamy skin and delicate colouring.

A minute to go. She suddenly came out of her trance and reached for a pair of low backless sandals before leaping across the room and out of the door as though the devil himself were after her. She didn't doubt for a moment that Luke was quite capable of following through on his outrageous threat, and although she was changed now, and quite decent, she didn't want to be alone with him in such intimate surroundings. In fact she didn't want to be *alone* with him at all, she thought ruefully. He seemed to have the knack of making her do exactly what she didn't want to do.

When she reached the pool area she thought at first that Luke wasn't there, until he called her name from where he was stretched out in idle relaxation on a cushioned sun lounger, his hands behind his head and dark glasses shading his eyes from the sun's powerful rays.

'A minute or two late, but I won't hold that against you.' He took the glasses off as he spoke, and then became quite still in much the same way she had a few moments earlier. 'You look beautiful,' he said softly. 'Very beautiful. Those colours suit you.'

'Thank you.' She was suddenly very conscious of the open shirt revealing the bikini top as his eyes lingered for a moment on the soft swell of her breasts against the silk, and was then absolutely mortified as she felt her body respond to the heavy-lidded stare.

She jerked the loose folds of cloth around her middle as she plumped down on the sun lounger next to his, but her breasts were still straining against the thin material, their points hard and aroused as the hot tide of sensation she had no defence against washed over her in waves of awareness. 'I— It's still very warm,' she muttered weakly, hoping he would attribute the heat in her cheeks to the sun's golden rays.

'Yes, it is.' She glanced at him then. His tone had been gentle, tender almost, with none of the caustic mockery of the afternoon. 'Have you put any suncream on?' he asked softly.

'What?' For a moment his words didn't register over the panicky beating of her heart, and then she took a deep breath and prayed for composure. 'Oh, no, no, I haven't, but it's nearly half past five. The sun won't be a problem now, will it?'

'In July the sun still burns out here until dusk,' he said quietly, 'but I have some here for you.' He reached by the side of his lounger and lifted a bottle, unscrewing the cap as he did so. 'Take the shirt and trousers off,' he said calmly, 'and I'll rub some on.'

He'd do what? The blood rushed and pounded in her ears, but the knowledge that she had already made a fool of herself in more ways than one that day gave her the strength to slip out of the clothes with a casual elegance that suggested she was used to near-naked men rubbing her with oil every day of the week. She lay face-down on the lounger, gritting her teeth as she nerved herself for his touch.

Her skin was hot but his hands were slow and cool as he smoothed the first drops of lotion into her tense back, his touch rhythmic and deliberately caressing. She wanted, she *really* wanted to remain oblivious to what his nearness and the slow, stroking action of his hands were doing to her, but it was no good. Even with her eyes tightly closed and her lips pressed together, little trickles of fire were flowing under his skilful fingers, creating havoc wherever they ran—and they were running pretty far, she thought desperately as her lower stomach began a dull throbbing that was both pain and pleasure.

He took his time working the sun-warmed liquid into every inch of her back, and by the time he had finished she felt fluid beneath his subtle fingers, the world closing in until it was just the two of them in the golden darkness behind her closed lids.

When he began on the sensitive silky skin of her upper legs she almost moaned out loud, before biting her lip so hard that it hurt, his sensual stroking of her soft flesh more voluptuous than she could ever have imagined. How did he know? she asked herself helplessly as waves of mingled pleasure and desire had every nerve-end pulsing. How did he know exactly where to touch her to make her flesh quiver? She couldn't stand it, not without giving herself away. She just couldn't . . .

The caress moved slowly to the delicate, tender area behind her knees, and she was unable to suppress the slight moan which his fingers drew forth. The lazy eroticism was shockingly sweet, and although she knew it was a cleverly planned strategy, another ploy he had no doubt used many times before with equal effect, she was helpless to prevent what it was doing to her body.

He had risen from his kneeling position at her side to sit on the edge of the lounger at some time during the proceedings, and now, as he bent and stretched across her pliant form, on the pretext of smoothing more lotion into the vulnerable area at the back of her neck, she became aware that he was hugely aroused.

This was fire. She was playing with fire. All the warnings were there but, blanketed by a wave of desire so strong, she had no defence against it.

'Right, turn over...' His voice was thick and husky and she shivered at the sound of it. He was breathing hard and she knew, without opening her eyes, that he was willing her to open herself to him. And she wanted to...

The thought should have shocked her out of the sensual lethargy that had taken hold but it didn't. She wanted him. She might regret it bitterly in the days ahead—in fact it was almost a sure-fire bet, she thought dizzily—but at this moment in time all she wanted was for his hands and mouth to continue the magic his touch had already created.

'Josie, turn over...'

And it was just as she began to move, her eyes opening the merest crack, that Madame Marat's weighty voice cut into the moment like a knife through butter. *'Monsieur?'*

The area where Luke had positioned the sun loungers was in a semi-circle completely surrounded by flowering bushes, which was why she had been unable to see him when she had first arrived. The pattern was repeated at intervals round the pool's edge, and they were completely hidden from the housekeeper's view. Nevertheless, Josie shot back as though she had been burned, her face scarlet, as Luke swore once, very explicitly, before straightening.

'Yes?' His voice was cold.

'*Pardon, monsieur.*' There followed a spate of words in rapid French before Luke stood up slowly, after wrapping a towel around his lean hips.

'I'll be there shortly.' Josie heard the sound of Madame Marat's large feet clicking away, but she hadn't opened her eyes throughout the conversation and didn't now. 'I have an urgent call from the States I've been waiting for,' Luke said softly to her rigid back. 'I won't be long.'

'Fine.' Her voice was muffled against the cushions and there was a moment's silence before he spoke again.

'Josie—'

'Please. Go and take the call.' She still kept her hot face buried, and it wasn't until she heard him pad away that she dared move.

How could she? How could she have come so near to—? To what? she asked herself faintly. Probably just a kiss. He had probably only wanted a kiss. But then she shook her head at her own naïvety. Men like Luke Hawkton didn't stop at a kiss in a situation like the one they had been in and she knew it.

She was stupid. So, so stupid. How could she have succumbed to such an obvious seduction attempt? she asked herself blindly as burning humiliation set her whole body aflame. But it had failed. More through luck than judgement, she admitted painfully as she swung her legs over the lounger and put her head in her hands. Nevertheless, it *had* failed. And she would make sure it wasn't repeated.

By the time Luke returned she was in the pool enjoying some serious swimming, the silky water cooling her body and bringing reason where madness had prevailed.

'You swim very well.' He stood at the side of the pool looking down at her in the water, his dark face smiling, and she forced herself to respond lightly, as though neither of them was aware of what had so nearly happened.

'My father taught me at a very early age. In view of our fishing expeditions he considered it essential that I could at least stay afloat if the boat overturned.'

'You do more than stay afloat,' he said approvingly, before diving into the blue depths himself, his lean, powerful body cutting through the water effortlessly as he came to her side. She had half expected him to follow up on his advantage, but he made no move to touch her, merely swimming at her side as they covered lap after lap of the massive pool, his muscled shoulders tanned and dark.

She tired long before he did, climbing out of the pool and pulling the shirt and trousers on over her damp bikini before she lay down on the sun-warmed lounger. The evening was scented and warm as it closed about her in a drowsy comfort that made her limbs heavy.

She must have slept, although she wasn't aware of it until a firm, warm mouth closed over hers, bringing her awake in an instant, and she jerked up so suddenly that the top of her head caught Luke a resounding bang on his chin.

'Ow...' He rubbed his jaw ruefully, flinging himself down on the lounger next to her and turning on one elbow to look into her flushed face. 'Do you always react like that when you're kissed?' he asked with a wry smile.

'Not always.' Her voice was uncertain, breathless, and she heard it with a stab of contempt. That was *not* the way to handle a man like Luke, but unfortunately the flush that had begun at the bottom of her feet had now reached her face, and all because she couldn't tear her eyes away from the flagrantly male body in front of her. Droplets of water were lingering on the brown skin, giving his body the texture of oiled silk, and the big frame was perfectly honed and lean, without an ounce of fat to be seen.

'In that case could we try again?' he said softly as he stood up.

'Luke—'

'Just a kiss, nothing more.' He pulled her up against him, feeling her tense in his arms, but his mouth was light on hers, the kiss fleeting, and perversely, even though she knew it was crazy, it left her wanting more. Which was probably part of the strategy, she thought tensely as he put her from him with a slight sigh, reaching for his robe on the lounger. 'It wasn't planned, you know...'

'What?' She watched him warily as he pulled the robe on and tightened the belt with a force that spoke of concealed frustration.

'Earlier.' He flicked his damp head at the lounger at her feet. 'You've been thinking it was a devious plan to have my wicked way with you, haven't you?'

'No!'

In spite of her vehemence he smiled crookedly, his eyes narrowing. 'Don't ever play poker, Josie—you'd lose the shirt off your back.' He took her arm and they left the pool area, his hand warm under her elbow. 'Mind you, you are right in thinking I want you,' he said conversationally as they walked back towards the house.

'I beg your pardon?'

'And don't act as if it's new to you.' He looked down at her, dainty and tiny at his side. 'In fact, if I'm being honest—and I'm always honest in situations like these—I can't remember when I've wanted a woman more than I want you.'

'Am I supposed to feel flattered?' she asked tightly. 'Because if so I can tell you that the thought of being another number in your little black book doesn't appeal.'

'I don't have one.' He stopped and drew her round to face him as he grasped her other elbow. 'I mean I *really* don't have one. I don't know what you've been hearing about me—'

'Red Riding Hood and her long-toothed friend?' she suggested flatly. 'Something along those lines? And don't act as if it's new to *you*,' she added with a heavy dose of sarcasm, 'because you must know that people talk.'

'I've always treated that as an occupational hazard until now,' he said grimly. 'I don't care who has told you what, but there are certain rules I adhere to both in my personal life and in business, OK? I'm always totally honest about what I want, I never welch on a deal and I never play anyone for a monkey. Do you believe that?'

'I—' The dusk air was sweet and heavy and perfumed with a thousand summer scents, and in spite of herself she felt the insidious power that he held draw her to him. It didn't help that the water had allowed his hair, short as it was, to curl slightly, giving his harsh face a softer, more boyish look that was totally at odds with everything she knew about him. 'Do you have your hair so short because it tends to curl?' she asked suddenly, as the thought occurred to her, the words popping out of her mouth before she could hold them back.

'What?' The silver eyes narrowed in blank astonishment. His hair was clearly the last topic he had expected to discuss.

'Your hair.' She reached up and touched a tiny wave before she realised how intimate the gesture was and jerked her hand away sharply. 'It looks quite different tonight.'

He gazed down at her for a full ten seconds before a small smile touched the hard line of his lips. 'It does curl,' he admitted, with a faintly sheepish air that did something crazy to her heartbeat. 'I've been trying to beat it since I was a boy. John and I used to get teased unmercifully at school, and we persuaded our mother to let us have it cut shorter than was the fashion then. I guess it's become a habit to have it short. Why? Don't you like it?' he added intently, the smile gone.

'Of course. It suits you,' she said hastily, wishing she had never brought the subject up as she turned and continued walking again, Luke falling into step by her side and suiting his long stride to her smaller one. But at least it had defused what had had the potential of being an acutely embarrassing moment.

He hadn't needed to tell her he wanted her; she knew that, she thought bleakly. But wanting wasn't loving—or even liking, she corrected quickly, horrified at the way her thoughts had swung. She didn't want Luke to love her, *of course* she didn't, she affirmed quietly in her mind, but mutual respect and friendship had its place in an intimate relationship, surely? Or else the human race were little better than animals.

She wished she hadn't come here. As they reached the house, still without exchanging another word, the thought was hot and fierce in her mind. He lived in a different world from her, with different values, rules, principles... But then even if he hadn't, even if he'd been a perfectly ordinary man who was looking for more than a casual affair, what difference would it have made? Either way it was no go, for her.

She glanced at him, smiling her thanks as he held the door open for her to walk into the house, and she recognised hunger in the silver-grey eyes. She turned away quickly. No, she shouldn't have come, but she had had no choice. All she could do now was be strong. She had been strong for the last thirteen years; it shouldn't be so very difficult now...

CHAPTER SEVEN

DINNER was another gastronomic treat, and as Josie finished the last of her dessert, a sweet batter pudding called *clafoutis* that was crammed with fruit and, Luke informed her lazily, a specialty of the Limousin region where Marie, the cook, had been born, she stretched slowly like a small and very satisfied cat.

'It's a wonder you aren't as fat as a pig,' she said lightly as she caught Luke's amused glance across the table. They were sitting on the veranda again, at her request. 'I would be if Marie was my cook.'

'If Marie was your cook that would mean you would be my wife, and I would not allow you to get fat,' Luke said smoothly as he poured them both a cup of coffee from the tray Josephine had just brought to the table. 'Except when you were with child, of course, and even then I would monitor your progress carefully.'

'You don't like plump women?' she asked carefully as the training of years prevented any pain from showing.

'I like plump women, thin women, tall women, short women,' he replied easily, 'as long as they are what suits them. But being fat would not suit you, Josie; you are too tiny, too fragile. You would look like...'

'A barrel?' she suggested drily as he paused for thought.

'Not at all.' He actually looked shocked.

'Well, don't worry.' She accepted her coffee with a nod of thanks, the aromatic wisp of steam from the cup rich and satisfying. 'With the sort of crazy job I've got I burn up the calories as soon as I've swallowed them, so no doubt I'll go into middle age with my figure intact.' Her meaning was clear and he stared at her for a long moment before indicating the quiet gardens beyond the rose bower.

'Drink that and we'll go for a wander down to the beach. It isn't dark yet, and the water looks wonderful on an evening like this as the light fades.'

'Does it?' She wasn't aware that both her voice and her face adequately expressed her apprehension, and when Luke laughed, a harsh, almost violent sound in the quietness, she started visibly.

'Don't do me any favours, Josie,' he said brutally as he watched her colour rise until her cheeks were bright pink. 'I'd hate to think there was any danger of you actually enjoying yourself in my company.'

'That's not fair—'

'The hell it isn't,' he said grimly, before standing up, moving round to her chair and hauling her out of her seat and into his arms before she could find breath to object.

He was angry. Very angry. That much registered as his mouth ground down on hers with a harshness that made her arch away from him, but she was far too tiny to make any impression on the hard steel of his body, and he subdued her effortlessly as he drew her even deeper into him, moulding her against him as he ran his hands down her shape with ruthless disregard for her struggles. And then his mouth softened, the punishing kiss turning into something hot and sensual as he groaned deep in his throat.

No, no, this can't be happening, she told herself frantically as she felt that sweet, consuming flood of sensation take hold of her again, weakening her resolve to fight and turning her legs to jelly. 'I hate you,' she muttered helplessly as his mouth moved to her throat, his lips burning her flesh with thrills of desire.

'No, you don't...' His lips returned to her mouth, probing the sweet moisture within as her lips opened to receive him in spite of herself. 'You want me. You might not like it, or me, but you want me as badly as I want you, and that's not hate.'

He kissed her again, fiercely and with a fire that sent trembling shivers down her spine, until she was soft and shaking against him. Her arms moved up to his broad shoulders and she hung on to him in a world that was pure sensation. She could feel the hard thrust of his arousal against her softness and she was both terrified and thrilled, her breath coming in sobbing pants against his mouth.

She had never understood, never dreamed that a man could wield such complete power by the touch of his hands, his mouth. It had been beyond her comprehension and was all the more shockingly exciting now because of all the closeted years when she had been unawakened.

Luke was breathing hard, and she could feel the trembling in her body reflected in the tremors that were sweeping his own as he cupped one full breast in his hand. Dragging his mouth from hers, he groaned again. 'I can't believe what you do to me, Josie.'

He stroked her skin through the soft silk of her dress, and she had to bite her lip until she tasted blood to stop herself moaning out loud as his fingertips brushed against the swollen, tender nipple, which was engorged and hard and hungry for more than the touch of his fingers.

'You're so perfect, so beautifully perfect...'

Perfect? She froze, an icy dread snaking over the heat that his touch had aroused and freezing it in its path. So he thought she was perfect? And she had let him think that, revelled in his touch, behaved as though she was free to offer more...

She had wrenched herself from his grasp before she finished thinking, turning and running swiftly from the veranda with a suddenness that took him completely by surprise. She heard him call her name once, his voice husky and broken, but she didn't stop until she reached the sanctuary of her room, falling through the door and locking it behind her before she collapsed onto the thick, soft carpet in an agony of pain and shock.

Perfect. The word stuck in her throat and reverberated in her head with a noise that was deafening. He thought she was perfect. She lay there for long minutes without moving, her face wet with tears that were hot and acidic. And that was why he wanted her. Why a man as rich and powerful and magnetic as Luke Hawkton had even spared her a second glance. Because the outward shell had fooled him. Had convinced him that she was a real woman...

'I am, *I am* . . .' She fought back against the cruel, merciless voice in her head, shocked that it had reared up with such a vengeance when she hadn't thought such damning thoughts for years. She *was* a real woman, she told herself painfully. She might not be able to have children, to conceive and bear fruit from male seed, but that didn't make her any less *herself*. Her intellect, her inner self, her personality, her soul—all those facets that made the whole— were still unimpaired and alive.

And a man like Luke Hawkton? the voice questioned ruthlessly. A man with a double dose of everything that made a man a man? Virile, magnetic, seductive, with a vigorous masculinity that was so powerful it was almost tangible? A man who had already stated that he would expect an heir as his right? How would a man like that view her searing defect?

She sat up slowly, wrapping her arms round her knees as she gazed blindly ahead. She had to stop doing this— resurrecting the fears and doubts and sense of failure that had almost crushed her thirteen years ago. They had no place in her life now. She could function exceptionally well in the world she had chosen and she was good at what she did; the fact that she was here after winning such a prize as the *Night Hawk* promotion proved it.

She had made a mistake in letting herself respond to Luke and doubled it when she'd let him become aware of the attraction he held for her. From now on she had to be aware of her weakness where he was concerned at every moment; that was where she had gone wrong before. She had trusted in her own strength, the resolve that had carried her for the last thirteen years, but all that didn't count where Luke was concerned.

For some reason he could cut through her defences with a single word, a glance, and she had to be on her guard every second she was around him. Because she wouldn't be able to bear him knowing the truth. That, above everything else she had gone through, would finish her.

The next day was another of brilliant sunshine, and when Josie awoke after what had virtually been one or two hours' sleep she stretched lazily under the pale green sheets as white sunlight poured into the room.

Her somnolent drowsiness ended abruptly as the events of the night before hit her mind and brought her bolt-upright in the big bed. *Luke*... Her heart began to thud and race and she forced herself to take several long, slow, deep, calming breaths before climbing out of bed and padding across to the bathroom.

It was still only half past six in the morning, and breakfast wasn't until eight, but as she stood under the warm shower with her face raised to the silky flow of water she felt she would need all of that time to prepare herself for the moment when she would have to face him again. She groaned softly at the thought. Those silver-grey eyes could be devastating at the best of times, and this—this was definitely *not* the best of times.

By the time she went down to breakfast, clothed in a short-sleeved coffee-coloured shirt and matching cotton skirt that ended two or three inches above her ankles, she had her nerves under control. Her hair was in a knot at the back of her head and secured with a clip from which not one curl dared escape, her make-up was tasteful and chic, and the gold studs in her tiny ears and fine gold bracelet on her wrist all proclaimed the same thing. She was in charge of her life and her destiny; she knew exactly where she was going and what she wanted.

In short, she was in control. The fact that she felt like melted jelly inside didn't matter, she told herself tightly as she walked into the large breakfast room that Josephine directed her to. No one could see that.

'Good morning, Josie.' Luke's face was expressionless as he glanced up from his newspaper, his voice cool but pleasant. 'Punctual as always. Top Promotions really are fortunate to have such a paragon of virtue.'

She met his eyes then, forcing herself to begin the speech she had rehearsed the night through. Twenty-eight-year-old unattached businesswomen didn't usually bolt like startled rabbits if a member of the opposite sex kissed them; she knew that. She also knew that she could have put a stop to things going so far weeks ago, right back in Germany, but... But somehow she couldn't send the right signals where Luke was concerned. Red turned to green with the lift of just one sardonic black eyebrow. So...she was partly to blame for this ridiculous situation, but it had to be dealt with right now, once and for all.

'Luke, last night was a mistake, and I think we need to discuss it,' she said quickly, before Josephine or Madame Marat appeared on the scene. 'If you feel it would be better if someone else from Top Promotions took over now I have no objection—'

'Josie—' The expressionless mask had lifted abruptly.

'No, please let me finish. We're two grown adults—'

He rose swiftly, cutting off her voice as he did so, and she raised her head as he moved to stand in front of her, peering down into her face with the strangest look on his.

'*One* of us is a grown adult,' he said softly, 'but I'm not quite sure what I am this morning. I should have been the one to clear the air and I should have apologised for my behaviour as soon as you walked in the room; it was inexcusable.'

She was too surprised to say anything. Whatever she had expected this morning it hadn't been this.

'But instead I retreated behind sarcasm, for which I must also apologise,' he continued. 'You did nothing wrong yesterday; the fault was mine and I have no wish that you should cease working on the *Night Hawk* project. The whole concept is yours and I want you to see it through to the end—the bitter end if necessary,' he added grimly.

As she stared up at him her heart gave a weird little jerk, the sense of confusion and agitation she always felt in his presence increasing tenfold. Why couldn't he be arrogant, contemptuous, cold—all the aspects of his character she had seen plenty of over the last few weeks? she asked herself. The biting mockery and cool derision that he put across so well she could have coped with, albeit painfully. She needed to keep the picture she had of him clear in her mind—that of ruthless tycoon and callous philanderer—but Luke Hawkton the man kept getting in the way here in his own little domain, where he seemed different somehow, more... human.

The panic increased and gave her voice a sharp, icy edge of self-protection. 'Very well. If you prefer me to see the project through to completion then of course I will. You are the boss, after all.'

There was a moment of complete and utter silence after she had dropped her eyes from his, her heart pounding so hard she felt physically nauseous, and then Josephine came bustling into the room with a trolley loaded with several covered dishes of hot food, a plate of freshly baked croissants, preserves, cold smoked ham, cheeses and a pot of steaming coffee.

Luke pulled out Josie's chair for her and she slid into it without speaking, knowing her cheeks were fiery and feeling as bad as if she had just slapped his face. Which, metaphorically speaking, she had, she admitted miserably. Dammit.

But she couldn't have done anything else. She had to hit this thing hard on the head, and if that involved making herself look like an ungracious, bad-tempered shrew then so be it. A man like Luke could have any woman he wanted; he wouldn't waste any more time on her after this. Which was exactly what she wanted... Wasn't it? *Yes*. Yes, yes, yes. The silent repetition was a valiant try but it failed miserably.

They ate breakfast in a silence Luke didn't even try to break, but as Josie forced down the last mouthful of her croissant, the hot dishes being quite beyond her with her stomach swirling in such an agony of apprehension, he suddenly spoke crisply into the charged atmosphere. 'The appointment with the caterers is at half past nine and the builders will be here at eleven to look at the site and your plans, so if you're ready...?'

'Yes, of course.' She wanted to put out her hand and touch him, to tell him that she appreciated what the apology had cost him in pride and dignity, but to do so would be to court disaster and she knew it.

The caterers' kitchens were immaculate and shining, their administration efficient and smooth and their expertise undeniable. After asking a few pertinent questions, to which she received the right replies, Josie settled down to working out the ins and outs of their requirements, and by the time she and Luke left, at exactly half past ten, she was more than satisfied that she had chosen well.

'You're very good at what you do, aren't you?' They were seated in Luke's low, powerful Aston Martin—she had learned that he had several different cars for virtually every occasion at the château—and travelling at some speed along the winding coastal road towards his estate.

'I could say the same about you,' she said lightly, without turning to look at him. He was dressed casually, in a black silk shirt and jeans, and she had felt weak all morning. The beautiful car didn't exactly detract from his image either, she thought silently, but then nothing would. He had it all.

'Yes, you could, but I was talking about you,' he said smoothly. 'Do you always check each detail yourself when you deal with a proposal?'

'Uh-huh.' She nodded as she risked a glance at the hard, tanned profile and then wished she hadn't as she caught a whiff of spicy, sensual aftershave. 'I've found it pays to leave nothing to chance. Even the firms that come with the best recommendations don't always match up to their reputation. It's better to trust no one.'

'Is it...?' The silver eyes narrowed and she wished she had worded that last comment differently. He had a way of picking up on what she said that was disconcerting.

'I think so.' She kept her voice very flat and matter-of-fact, as though she thought they were discussing only her attitude to her work. 'Face-to-face contact is good too, for both sides. They can see I won't tolerate any slackness for one thing. It's amazing how many male-oriented firms still think they know better than a mere woman.'

'And do they?' he asked drily.

'Occasionally.' She nodded slowly. 'Yes, occasionally, but that's no problem. I'm always open to good suggestions.'

'I wish.'

Josie expelled a quiet breath, conscious that the silver-grey gaze had flashed swiftly over her face.

'You don't flirt, do you?' he asked softly, making the words more of a statement than a question. 'Not at all. I find that very... refreshing, but also very disturbing.'

'Disturbing?' She turned fully to him now, sensing and resenting criticism.

'You are young, beautiful, successful and excellent at what you do. With most women one of those attributes would guarantee a certain... confidence. But you aren't confident, Josie, not deep inside, where it really counts. So, yes, I do find that disturbing,' he finished expressionlessly. 'More than disturbing.'

'I don't know what you're talking about.' Her voice was too high and too sharp and she tried to moderate it, her stomach turning over in panic. 'Really, Luke, you do seem determined to make a drama where none exists.'

'Don't I?' he agreed complacently. 'But, you see, I've learnt at least one thing during our short acquaintance, and that is that you never say what you mean. Now, with my vast experience of women—' the hard mouth twisted sardonically '—I'm used to that regrettable little defect to a greater or lesser extent as par for the course. But you're different.' He paused and the butterflies in her stomach went into overdrive.

'With you that defect is not used as an easy way out, part of the male-to-female game to keep me guessing and interested, to titillate and intrigue. Your dishonesty is honest. You would like me to flatter and appreciate your beauty and your gracefulness, like any other woman would, but you don't ask for it—not by word or gesture or even from the depths of those great honey-gold eyes. Why?'

'Why?' She was trembling deep in her stomach at the sudden confrontation, and terrified, more than terrified, at the thought of where it would lead.

'Yes, why?' he repeated slowly. 'If it wasn't so crazy, so ridiculous, I'd think you didn't rate yourself at all, but one look in the mirror would blow that theory to hell. So what is it that keeps you behind that locked door? And don't say it's where you want to be because I won't buy it. Last night you wanted me, Josie; you wanted me so badly I could taste it, feel it, smell it—but it wasn't enough. *Dammit!*'

There was a thread of anger in his voice now, a rage that she couldn't guess was directed at himself rather than her. 'Why wasn't it enough? How could you let someone stop you living, loving—?'

'I haven't—'

'Don't give me that.' His voice was too hard, and as she flinched he cursed himself for letting his frustration show. Force wouldn't get her out of that steel prison; she'd just retreat further from him again. 'Josie, it's only a man that *could* make you withdraw from life like you have. What did he do? Beat you? Ill-use you? Or was it some form of mental cruelty, is that it? However much you loved him, however it went wrong, can't you see you're still the winner? You are young and beautiful and desirable and it's his loss, not yours. If he didn't value what he had then you're better off without him—'

'Please—please, Luke . . .' She couldn't take any more of this. Winner? He thought she was a winner? The bitter irony swept through her with such intensity that she felt faint for a moment. He saw what the world saw. What would he say if he saw the real Josie Owens?

'OK, OK.' He held up one large, tanned hand as he accelerated with more fury than finesse, the powerful car leaping forward with a growl of rage. 'But it's a waste. A damn waste.'

You'll never know how much of one, she answered him silently as misery became a hard lump in her throat.

The scenery was flashing by the windows as the car fairly flew along the road. They were back at the château in half the time it had taken them to drive to the caterers, arriving a moment before an impressive dove-grey Mercedes, which drew to a smooth halt just as Luke opened Josie's door.

'Mr Hawkton?' The tall, burly, fair-haired man who unwound himself from the car's interior was handsome and young, his good-looking face wreathed in a smile that didn't fade an iota at Luke's less than enthusiastic response. 'I'm Pierre Delpire; I have an appointment with yourself and a Miss Owens at eleven.'

He spoke excellent English, Josie thought fleetingly as she smiled and shook hands with the young Adonis along with Luke, his accent adding just a faint sexy tinge to his words. And he was the first builder she had met who travelled in a Mercedes, she reflected wryly, although this *was* the South of France after all.

'I expected someone older.' Luke's voice was not exactly offensive but it wasn't welcoming either, and the other man's hundred-watt smile dimmed slightly as it met the silver-grey gaze.

'Did you?' Pierre Delpire was polite, but clearly he felt somewhat out of his depth. 'Probably my father. But he would not be of use on something like this, Mr Hawkton, not at this stage. I have trained as an architect and so we decided it would be useful if I came to discuss the preliminaries, yes? Then if the proposition is feasible we go from there?'

Luke looked set to argue some more, but before he could speak Josie nodded brightly, her voice brisk. 'That's fine, Monsieur Delpire. Perhaps you'd like to come and look at the site?'

'Thank you, yes.' He smiled down at her, the bright intensity back in shining order as his vivid blue eyes took in the delicate beauty of the small woman in front of him.

'Mr Hawkton has hired my firm to oversee the project,' Josie said quietly as the three of them passed through the massive wrought-iron gate at the side of the house that led directly into the gardens. 'The idea of the ice rink was mine, so I would be grateful for any help you can give that will make things easier.'

'Although you will, of course, be dealing directly with me most of the time,' Luke put in smoothly, taking her elbow in a firm grip as they walked. 'That is understood?'

'Of course, Mr Hawkton.' The other man seemed mildly puzzled by Luke's cold voice, and Josie had to bite back the sudden burst of anger his authoritative tone brought to the surface. He was acting as though he didn't think she was capable of overseeing the work, she thought tightly, when he knew quite well that wasn't true.

'You speak excellent English.' She forced every trace of annoyance from her voice as she smiled up at Pierre when an awkward silence had reigned for a few moments. He was a good few inches smaller than Luke, although the hard, firm body was muscular and fit, his face clear and unlined.

'I lived in England with my mother for ten years, until I was twenty-five,' the young Frenchman explained quietly. 'When she died my father offered me a place in his business, so I moved out here two years ago. I love France, my father's country, but I also love England.' He smiled at her, his face open and friendly. 'An English country pub on a warm summer evening with the smell of woodsmoke in the air is hard to beat.'

'Where did you live?' she asked interestedly, unaware of Luke's dark, frowning face at her side.

'Sussex. A little village called Oakcross.'

'I know Oakcross,' she said delightedly, before she could think. 'I—' The sudden realisation that she had said more than she intended came too late. 'I lived near there at one time,' she added weakly.

'Did you?' Pierre grinned down at her. 'We will have to compare notes—' He came to an abrupt halt. 'Owens— Josie Owens. I knew I recognised the name from somewhere. You were with Peter Staples when he had that first car crash of his, weren't you?'

'Peter?' She too had stopped, and she turned to face the young Frenchman, aware as she looked at him of Luke's keen glance on them both. 'I . . . yes, I—I knew Peter when I was younger,' she stammered weakly. Here, of all places, to be faced with the past. It was ironic, bitterly ironic, she thought desperately. How much did Pierre know, and how quickly could she change the subject?

'You know he is dead?' The words were stark, and without any of the social niceties that were normal in such a conversation.

'Dead?' She stared at Pierre, her eyes enormous in the whiteness of her face. 'No. No, I didn't know that,' she said numbly, shock at the sudden revelation freezing any other reaction.

'Another crash similar to the one with you,' Pierre said levelly, his face straight now. 'He was a good friend, your Peter. The parties and fun we had . . . He—how do you say it?—took me under his wing when I arrived in England. Showed me the good time...'

He would, Josie thought silently as her mind whirled and spun. Even when she had known him, and especially after the crash, his friends had begun to drift away, recognising the true personality of the man they had hero-worshipped. Peter would have loved having a good-looking young man like Pierre in tow, to bolster the playboy image that had begun to tarnish, and it was clear that he had completely taken in Pierre with that synthetic charm he'd practised so well.

'He wrapped his car round a tree,' Pierre continued flatly, 'after he'd been drinking. He drank a lot after that crash with you—but then I suppose you know about that. And the women... He was always searching for understanding. If you hadn't left him like that—'

'Like what?' Josie stared at Pierre in amazement. What on earth had Peter told the young Frenchman? It was clear from his face that he held her personally responsible for his hero's death.

'You broke his heart—'

'I did nothing of the sort,' Josie flashed back as she found her tongue along with a furious rage that burnt in every nerve and sinew. So that was how Peter had explained to everyone the circumstances of that first horrific crash, with its tragic consequences? Holding himself up as a remorseful, rejected suitor whose woman had walked out on him when he'd needed her most?

'It wasn't his fault, you know,' Pierre said sorrowfully. 'He always wished he could have convinced you of that—'

'*Were you there?*' Josie bit out tightly. 'Were you? No, you weren't. So just keep quiet about something you know nothing about.'

'I—'

'I think Miss Owens is saying the matter is closed.' If Luke's voice had been any colder the air around them would have splintered, and Pierre suddenly seemed to realise where he was and why. 'Now, if you'd care to continue with the job you are going to be paid a great deal to do...' Luke continued icily, and he waved a hand for them to start walking again.

'Of course.' Pierre was now a deep scarlet, but Josie couldn't dredge up any sympathy for the young man as Luke once more took her arm in a firm hold. The past was suddenly more real than the present, all the pain and agony and terrible desperation of that time at the forefront of her mind as she walked between the two men to the site of the proposed ice rink.

How *dared* Peter play the part of the innocent? she asked herself angrily. How dared he? And how could anyone, *anyone* believe such a ridiculous story? But then Peter at his most charming had been hard to resist, and to a young, gullible French boy in a new country with no friends... Yes, she could see that Pierre must have been a sitting duck for Peter's strategy—like herself all those years ago.

So he was dead? Even as she discussed the ice rink plans and future arrangements a separate portion of her brain was ticking away on a different plane altogether. Peter Staples was dead. She waited for some emotion—anything—but it was as though all her feelings had fallen into a great vacuum.

In the early days after the accident, when she had been coping with the knowledge of her own mutilation and the fact that her father's death was due to that man, she had wished him dead constantly. And afterwards, even as she had begun to carve out her new life, she had been consumed by a wish for revenge, driven by it.

But now? Now all she felt was a faint sense of relief that no other woman would suffer the same kind of torment she had at Peter's hands. He had died as he had lived, violently and foolishly, and she was just glad that in his dying he hadn't taken anyone with him. He already had the deaths of two men to answer for.

Pierre left just before lunch, after the plans for the small but extremely expensive ice rink had been agreed, and Luke was in a dark mood of his own as the Mercedes drew away, the occupant clearly relieved to be leaving.

'Are you happy with the arrangements so far?' Josie asked tentatively as they walked into the house, breaking the icy silence. She had decided to endeavour to keep the conversation purely and solely on the job in hand if she could, although her instinct told her it was a forlorn hope.

'Ecstatic,' he said crisply without looking at her. 'Shouldn't I be?'

'If you don't like anything that has been mentioned you only have to say—'

'Really?' He cut into her careful words with all the softness of a bullet. 'Well, there was just one little thing, as it happens. How come an ape like that knows more about you than I do?'

'What?' She stared at him, unable to believe she was hearing right.

'And don't play dumb; it doesn't suit you. You know exactly what I am referring to, Josie. He knows about your past life, your old boyfriend—this Peter—and what is Pierre Delpire to you? Nothing. Absolutely nothing. But I'm left standing there like an old flame at a wedding. Oh, to hell with it—' He ground out the words through clenched teeth. 'What does it matter anyway?'

'But I don't know Pierre Delpire,' she said confusedly, utterly bewildered by the black rage darkening the rugged features.

'Exactly. He is a stranger to you, a complete stranger, yet he knows more about you than I do. How do you think that made me feel back there?' he said furiously, his eyes slits of silver.

'I . . . I don't understand—'

'*You* don't understand?' he snarled scathingly. 'It's damn clear I'm the one who doesn't understand anything. You were involved with this Peter, from all accounts, and then gave him the old heave-ho and drove the guy half-insane. What was it? The career beckoning? The bright lights of the city? Or did the poor fool want to marry you, have a family? That would really have done it, wouldn't it? Who are you, Josie? *What* are you? How can one woman give off so many different signals?'

'I don't have to explain myself to you or anyone else,' she said tightly, her face white.

'No, that's right—that's absolutely right,' he agreed, his face as black as thunder. 'You are your own person, aren't you? Answerable to no one and with no one answerable to you.'

'Yes.' She raised her chin and looked him full in the face as her heart thundered so hard she felt she was going to pass out at his feet. 'That's how it is.'

'And how you want it to remain?' he asked coldly.

She nodded, not trusting her voice, willing herself to remain in control for just a few moments more until she could make an excuse and escape that devastating gaze.

'I see. Well, there is really nothing more to be said, then, is there? If you will excuse me, I shall have lunch in my study while I work on some papers. You may have yours in your room or on the veranda, whichever you prefer.' He stared at her, the silver eyes like liquid mercury.

'Thank you,' she said woodenly, before turning and walking away, her heart cut to ribbons.

Later that afternoon, her face clear of the tearstains that ravaged her features earlier, after the disastrous confrontation with Luke, she stood down on the beach watching the dancing waves lit with sparkling sunshine, the hot, powdery sand like velvet beneath her bare feet.

She had worked for an hour after lunch, but an aching head and an aching heart had driven her outside after a while, and now her walk was slow and weary as she made her way back to the pool area. She had just settled herself on one of the loungers positioned under the dappled shade of a large cherry tree, when the sound of children's laughter brought her head jerking upright.

'*Oh, pardon, mademoiselle...*' As Madame Marat caught sight of her she came to a sudden stop, causing the trio of chattering children behind her to cannon into her back. 'I did not know you were 'ere,' she apologised hastily, and she turned to usher the now silent infants back the way they had come. 'We come back another day, *mademoiselle—pardon.*'

'Please, don't do that.' Josie felt highly embarrassed at spoiling what was obviously a treat for the housekeeper's grandchildren. 'I don't mind, really. I think the pool is big enough for everyone.' She smiled warmly into the Frenchwoman's forbidding countenance and received a tentative smile in return.

'Is no problem to come back another day,' Madame Marat said anxiously. 'They are a leetle noisy—excited, you know?'

'It's perfectly all right.' Josie was conscious of three pairs of wide blue eyes surveying her from under three curly mops of hair, and she forced herself to smile at the small children even as her heart gave the little twist that all such encounters caused. They were very pretty—unlike their grandmother—and very small. 'How old are they?' she asked Madame Marat quietly.

'Denis is nearly two.' She indicated a rosy-cheeked little boy, who grinned at Josie immediately. 'Maime is three and Françoise is four.'

'They're lovely children,' Josie said softly.

'They are an 'andful, *mademoiselle*.' Madame Marat grimaced dramatically. 'But is it any wonder? This is what I ask myself. Their *papa*, he run off—*poof*! You understand, *mademoiselle*? So now my poor daughter, she is all alone. Is very 'ard for 'er, I think?'

Josie nodded sympathetically even as she envied Madame Marat's luckless daughter from the bottom of her heart. With three beautiful babies like these their mother was rich in everything that mattered, she thought silently, although probably the poor woman couldn't see it that way right now.

'Well, please, let them play,' Josie said quietly.

'*Merci, mademoiselle.*' Madame Marat said something in rapid French to the three children, who immediately echoed their grandmother's thanks, their baby voices high and shrill. There was much giggling and chattering and several covert glances in Josie's direction as their grandmother blew up three pairs of armbands, but once in the water the little tots splashed about at the pool's shallow end while Madame Marat sat at the edge, dangling her feet, her voice raised in warning now and again if they ventured too far.

And after a while it happened . . . as it always did if Josie came into contact with children. Whether it was her hunger, her longing, her love for all children that drew them to her she didn't know, but, despite their grandmother's repeated admonishments, first one little wet body then another crept over to her side, and she found herself playing and talking with them despite the language barrier.

In the world she had chosen to live in she wasn't often put in such a situation, but on the rare occasions it happened the result was always the same; an immediate rapport and understanding. And a particular kind of exquisite torture for her.

And so it was, just as Madame Marat was trying to persuade them that they had to go home for tea, cajoling them with promises of further afternoons in the pool, that Luke found her, engulfed by tiny plump arms and legs and wriggling bodies, her face alight and her whole being absorbed in the little tots.

He stood and watched her for long minutes before he made his presence known—when the three children were leaving amid tears of protest—and, as he had expected, once she caught sight of him walking towards her the shutter snapped back into place with military precision. And he couldn't believe how angry it made him.

'Had a restful afternoon?' He kept his voice expressionless and cool, dropping down on the lounger next to her and stretching out his body to the sun's warmth after slipping off his towelling robe, his head turned to watch her face.

'Yes, thank you,' she lied quickly.

'With those three around?' He kept the disbelief light. 'They tire me out in an hour.'

She lowered her head, allowing the mass of silky curls to hide her flushed face. 'They are nice children,' she said flatly.

'Yes, they are.' He allowed a moment's pause, his eyes evaluating the tension evident in the strained posture of her arms and legs, in the rigid neck and shoulder muscles. 'Did Madame Marat tell you their father has left?' he asked evenly. 'Ran off with another woman, I understand.'

'Yes, she mentioned it.' This was awful; she wouldn't be able to work for him with the atmosphere so tense that the air was vibrating, Josie thought miserably. She'd have to apologise. 'Luke, about this morning—'

'Forget it,' he said shortly. 'I have. That's the best thing, isn't it?'

'I guess so.' She straightened, her head turning to the smooth blue expanse of shimmering water. 'I'm going to have a swim.'

'Good idea.' He didn't follow her immediately, watching for a few minutes as she forced her body through the water at a punishing pace, as though her life depended on it.

She didn't see his fluid dive into the pool but when he surfaced just in front of her, his arms reaching out almost in the same instant to draw her to him, she was too surprised to object. 'You're too serious about your swimming.' His eyes held hers tightly, their depths metallic. 'Don't you ever have fun?'

'Yes...' Her voice was breathless, but not through vigorous exercise. The feel of that hard male body next to hers, his furry coating of body hair coarse against her softness, was making coherent thought difficult.

'Prove it.' He kissed her once, very hard on the lips, before lifting her right out of the water and throwing her some feet away into the deeper part of the pool. When she emerged, gasping and spluttering, he was there beside her, grinning at her outraged expression.

'You could have warned me.' She glared at him, her hair a mass of tight red curls on which the drops of water sat like diamonds.

'I could have...' he agreed lazily.

And there began a crazy game of tag, the likes of which Josie hadn't enjoyed since she was a child. And quite when it happened she didn't know, but by the time they emerged from the water to lie on the sun-warmed loungers she knew...beyond all reasonable doubt. She loved him.

CHAPTER EIGHT

JOSIE must have slept in the warmth of the evening sun,
but some sixth sense suddenly brought her awake to find
herself staring straight into Luke's eyes where he lay propped
on his lounger watching her.

She couldn't remember falling asleep; she certainly hadn't
intended to as she had lain there stiff and taut, her mind
exploring endless possibilities and explanations that would
refute what her heart was telling her. She couldn't love him.
It was madness. And besides, she didn't want to—she didn't
want to love anyone, least of all Luke Hawkton. But...she
did. Helplessly. And certainly hopelessly.

'Sleeping Beauty...' He smiled lazily as his eyes stroked
over her face. 'There aren't many women who look more
beautiful without make-up, but you are one of them.'

'Very gallant but a definite exaggeration.' She smiled as
she spoke but her movements were jerky as she sat up, ad-
justing her bikini as she did so. The wet silk had folded in
on itself a little over her thighs, and was getting danger-
ously near the needle-thin scar at the bottom of her stomach.
Nothing could have reminded her more poignantly that any
attraction between herself and Luke was doomed. She
wouldn't survive a casual, light affair, but she couldn't ask
for more either.

'I don't think so.' That warmth in his eyes meant nothing,
she told herself brutally as she smiled again without
answering, rising from the lounger and slipping into the
sarong she had brought down with her then pushing her
damp hair away from her face. Nothing beyond lust,
anyway. 'You're retreating again.' His voice was very low
and very deep, and she shivered slightly as she forced herself
to look into his face. 'And after I was so magnanimous
about our...disagreement before lunch, too.'

146

'I'm sorry?' Her voice was cool and she blessed the strength that was coming from ... somewhere.

'Out there in the pool we had fun,' he said quietly. 'Didn't we?'

'Yes, but—'

'And now you're withdrawing again, going back into that steel-plated armour of yours.' There was a bite of anger in his voice that was reflected in the dark colour on his high cheekbones. 'Why? What the hell is it about me you find so hard to take anyway?'

'I don't find you hard to take, Luke,' she said carefully as her stomach lurched and spun. She needed time to convince herself that all this was just a mirage, time to persuade her heart to believe the lie that she didn't love him. She didn't need this sort of challenge right now. She should have known—she should have guessed what was happening to her weeks ago, guessed why she was so affected by him. Why hadn't she? Why on earth hadn't she? she asked herself bleakly. And it was too late now. Pandora's box had been opened.

'Sure you don't.' There was a rawness in his voice now that hit a nerve in her, causing her to flinch slightly, and, tiny though the movement was, he caught it and his rage increased. 'And don't do that either,' he ground out through clenched teeth as he too stood upright.

'Do what?' She was aware that his self-control was on a knife-edge, but quite how the sudden confrontation had erupted she wasn't sure; she only knew she had to keep calm and quiet.

'Cower away from me as though I'm some sort of wild animal,' he growled furiously. 'Damn it all, Josie, I've worn kid gloves for the last few weeks and still it's not enough. What the hell do you want from me anyway?

'Nothing.' *Everything*, her mind screamed desperately.

'Nothing.' He nodded slowly. 'Boy, you sure know how to make a man feel good about himself, don't you?' he said with an acidic cynicism that cut into her heart like a knife. 'But I don't think "nothing" is quite true, is it, sweetheart?' There was cruelty in both his voice and his face now, cruelty and something else that turned the dark male skin white under its tan. 'We both know what happens when I touch you, Josie. You might not like it, and I sure as hell know you're fighting it, but nevertheless you want me. Why can't you be satisfied with that as a beginning and we'll see how it goes—?'

'You mean sex,' she cut in painfully, her heart breaking. 'You want me for sex, mating—call it what you will. But anyone would do for that, as long as they've got the physical requirements—'

'Don't! Don't you dare relegate it to that!'

She turned away quickly, frightened by the darkness in his face, but he caught her wrist before she could take more than one step, spinning her round with a violence that spoke of his anger more adequately than words.

'Can't you see—?' He stopped abruptly, biting back what he had been about to say and taking a deep, calming breath before he spoke again, his hold on her wrist iron-hard. 'I'm a thirty-five-year-old man, Josie, not some schoolboy wet behind the ears and governed purely by what's between his legs. Do you understand me?' She stiffened at the crudity but he shook her slightly, his eyes glittering. 'Do you understand me?' he ground out tightly.

'Yes.' She tried to jerk herself free but his grip didn't lessen. 'Yes, yes, yes! Now let me go—'

'I know you don't like me pointing out that you want me physically, but it's a fact. Now, whether you've got some sort of twisted loyalty to some bozo who's let you down, or whether you've convinced yourself the only way to get to the top of the career tree is to be alone, I don't know. What I do know is that you aren't happy and I could fix that. I could make you live again.'

'I am living.' She had ceased trying to struggle; he wasn't giving an inch.

'The hell you are.' He was breathing hard, his powerful chest rising and falling as he towered over her like an avenging angel, and despite the danger he represented she couldn't hide what his near-naked body was doing to hers; her body was ripening and responding to this man she loved. 'The hell you are . . .'

His mouth was both fierce and tender, and the combination was wickedly sensual, as he had intended it should be, sweeping her into another dimension of touch and taste and smell. He kept up the assault until she was aware of nothing but him, little moans of pleasure trembling on her lips as he explored her throat and breasts, the silk of the sarong pushed aside by his searching mouth.

He was bent right over her as he curved her softness into his hard frame, his hands moving in slow, lingering caresses that fed the fever which had taken hold of every part of her until she was one mass of burning, aching desire, without mind or reason. He was hugely aroused, the brief black trunks he wore accentuating rather than concealing his ardour, but despite her innocence the thrust of his body was thrilling—frighteningly, unbelievably thrilling.

'You want me...' It was a hoarse statement against the warm softness of her skin. 'Say it. Say you want me.'

She heard herself say the words with a feeling of disbelief, but they came from her heart, born of her love. 'I want you...'

When he put her from him she didn't understand, not at first, not until she opened dazed eyes to look into his face. 'That's living,' he said thickly, a muscle jumping in his hard, square jaw as he took a step back from her. 'That and much, much more. But I don't want just your body, Josie; I want all of you. And I won't take you until I know I've got it all. You understand me?' he added with magnificent arrogance, his face dark and proud.

She couldn't answer him; she could barely stand, let alone talk. She just stared at him out of huge, bruised golden eyes and he swore softly under his breath when she didn't move or speak.

The walk back to the château through the beautiful grounds bathed in soft evening sunlight was conducted in a silence that was spiky and taut, and the only way Josie could cover the distance was by retreating into the stoical reserve she had developed over long, lonely years.

Was she wrong? She found she was doubting herself badly. Should she start a relationship with Luke? Do what her heart longed, craved to do, and let the future, whatever it might be, take care of itself?

He could have taken her then, down in the sheltered hideaway by the pool, with the blue sky above and the scent of summer all around. He knew it and she knew it. But he hadn't. He had stopped. Stopped after proving what they both knew—that she was his for the asking. So why, in the final analysis, *hadn't* he asked? Because he was interested in more than just a physical relationship? Her heart gave an enormous bound and lurched up into her throat. But that would make things worse, not better... wouldn't it?

'Ah, *monsieur*...' As they entered the massive hall Madame Marat had obviously just picked up the phone, and she held it out to Luke with a smile. 'It is Catherine, *monsieur*.'

'Thank you.' Whether he heard Josie's sudden intake of breath she didn't know, but he turned to her at the same moment that he grasped the telephone. 'She's phoning from England—you remember you met her?'

'Yes, I know who Catherine is.' She couldn't believe how calm and cool she sounded when she was dying inside.

'You do?' His eyes narrowed for a moment, but she kept her face quite expressionless with a will she'd never known she possessed. 'Oh, right.' Her calmness seemed to reassure him. 'Those wagging tongues again?' He didn't even seem concerned.

She had turned before he had even finished speaking, walking towards the stairs with careful measured steps on legs that threatened to let her down at any moment. He could kiss her like that, make love to her with such passion and tenderness, and then dismiss his girlfriend's calling with a casual phrase like 'those wagging tongues'? It was the answer to all her sudden doubts. His world could never be her world; it was as simple as that.

Dinner was an endurance test that she got through with gritted teeth and a good deal of precarious dignity, excusing herself immediately afterwards by pleading a headache and escaping to her room, where she stayed for the rest of the evening. She half expected Luke to come and find her, and the tension of waiting, of both hoping and fearing that he would come, had made the headache a reality by the time she crawled into bed just after midnight, only to lie awake most of the night, tossing and turning in an agony of grief and anguish for the loss of something she had never had.

Breakfast was a cool affair, with Luke aloof and unapproachable behind his newspaper after a cursory good morning and a sharp, penetrating glance at her white face and shadowed eyes.

The journey to the airport, the flight to England, the car ride through London to her flat—all were conducted in the same distant, remote silence, broken only by the necessities of communication that such travel warranted.

When they drew up outside the house Luke gestured to his chauffeur, who had been waiting at the airport, to remain in the car, and carried her suitcase himself, despite her insistence that she could manage.

The tall, commanding tycoon in the designer-cut suit and hand-made shoes seemed very different from the angry lover of the day before, and now, in the cold light of England, Josie couldn't believe that this millionaire ten times over had ever said he wanted her. Even the weather had changed; a damp, muggy drizzle was lowering the temperature a good few degrees and creating a feeling of gloominess. And she felt gloomy, more than gloomy—

'Your key?' They were standing outside her flat, and she came to with a start to realise that she had been miles away and immersed in dark thoughts of her own.

'I've got it. Yes, here it is.' She waved her doorkey in front of his face and forced a bright smile. 'Thank you so much for allowing me to stay in your beautiful home—'

'Open the door.' He cut into her little speech of thanks she had been rehearsing throughout the tense, strained journey home without blinking.

'Oh, it's all right, I can manage now—'

'The flat has been vacant for a couple of days and I would prefer to check everything is in order before I leave,' he said flatly. 'That's all. I have no intention of leaping on you, if that's what you're worried about.'

'It isn't.' It was true. With sultry seductresses like
Catherine around, charming temptresses who had no hang-
ups, no secrets, no inhibitions about letting him know they
thought he was the best thing since sliced bread, why would
he persevere with a head case like her? she thought dismally.

'Good. Open the door.' He eyed her expressionlessly, his
rugged dark face implacable and very, very remote.

The flat seemed tiny, minute, after the luxurious
spaciousness of the château, but it was home, and as Josie
glanced around her when she followed Luke through the
door she had to bite back the tears that had been hovering
behind her eyes since the fiasco of the evening before.

'Mog?' Normally the cat had an uncanny instinctive
knowledge of when she would be home, and she couldn't
remember a time when he hadn't been waiting to greet her,
but now even her call got no response.

'Everything seems in order.' Luke was back at her side
before she could call again. 'You'll get those invitations off
within the next day or so, then? You have the list my secretary prepared?'

'Yes.' He was leaving, just like that, without another
word? As though the fact that they had nearly become lovers
last night meant nothing at all to him? But perhaps it didn't.
She dredged up another bright smile that cost her more
than he would ever know. 'I'll do them this afternoon.'

'Right.' He nodded slowly, his eyes watching her with an
intensity she didn't understand. 'Goodbye, Josie.'

It sounded so final.

And then he walked out of the door, shutting it quietly
behind him.

When Mog still hadn't returned by nine o'clock that night,
thick panic began to replace the misery she felt over Luke.
She ventured down to Mr Jones's flat at nine-thirty, and
when he told her that he hadn't seen Mog for the last twenty-
four hours she felt sick. She had found a saucer of un-
touched food on the kitchen floor which Mr Jones confirmed he had left there the night before, not bothering to
replace it that morning because he had thought the cat had
been out for a night on the tiles.

'Which I think he still is, love,' the caretaker said comfortingly as Josie stared at him with worried eyes. 'He can look after himself, that one; there's no flies on him. He's a toughie, all right.'

But he wasn't tough where cars were concerned, Josie thought, and her stomach began a dance all of its own. Against steel and metal, sharp claws and bared teeth were no defence. In spite of Mr Jones's very verbal warnings, which encompassed everything from white-slave trading to being mugged, she began a search of the immediate area, combing the nearby streets and gardens, but with no success.

It was dark when she arrived back at the flat, and her heart was in her mouth when she opened the door, but there was no welcoming miaow or running paws, just an empty silence which hit her hard in the chest. 'Mog...' She didn't switch the light on, just padded across to the window and looked out over the shadowed streets where high-rise buildings in the distance illuminated the night sky with tiny squares of glowing warmth. 'Where are you, Mog?'

He was more than just a cat. He was her family. She hugged herself tight round her waist as she swayed back and forwards in the darkness. He had a collar on, with a little tag giving his name and address, but people didn't bother about other human beings in the city, she thought painfully. Would anyone take the trouble even to contact her if he was hurt or—? She shut her eyes tightly. He wasn't dead. She wouldn't believe he was dead.

When the phone rang a moment later she nearly jumped out of her skin before running to answer it, hope leaping in her breast. 'Yes?' she said breathlessly into the receiver.

'I've been ringing you since half past nine,' Luke said coldly, his voice harsh.

'Have you?' Her concern for Mog was such that it didn't even occur to her to take umbrage at the authoritative tone. 'I've been out.'

'Obviously,' he said with cutting coolness. 'Are you alone now?'

'Alone?' She found herself glancing round the flat before she pulled herself together. 'Yes—yes, I'm alone,' she said quickly. 'What's the matter?'

'My mother has produced a list of her own that needs incorporating with the original invitations,' Luke said tightly. 'I presume that will present no difficulty, or have you already sent the first batch out?'

'The first batch?' She thought she heard the catflap and jerked round, but it was only empty air that met her eyes. 'I... Sorry, what did you say?'

'Are you sure you haven't got anyone there?' he asked grimly. 'You seem ... preoccupied. I wouldn't want to intrude—'

'Mog's missing.' She knew her voice was too shrill, and tried to bring it down a tone. He already had every justification for thinking she was neurotic; what on earth was she telling him this for? A cat would mean nothing to a man like him—

'How long has be been gone?' he asked softly, all harshness leaving his voice.

'I... I'm not sure.' She heard the sob in her voice with a feeling of despair, but she couldn't help it. If he had been curt and uninterested she could have coped, but the sympathy in his voice was her undoing. 'Mr Jones was looking after him, as he usually does if I'm away, but Mog didn't have his food last night and he hasn't been back all day. He's never stayed out for more than a night before; he's not that sort of cat.'

'I'm sure he's not.' It wouldn't be until much later that she would remember the slight thread of amusement in his voice. 'Has anyone had a look round the neighbourhood?' There was the barest pause before his voice changed abruptly. 'That's where you've been, isn't it? Did Mr Jones accompany you?' he asked sharply.

'I— No. He's busy; he's got a friend staying the night and—'

'So you've been wandering about on your own?' Luke asked grimly.

'Look, I had to.' If he started a row now she would put the phone down, she thought desperately. 'He might be hurt—a car or something. Or those people who steal cats for their fur. Or—'

'I'm coming over.' She held the phone a fraction from her ear and stared at it in surprise, her mouth dropping open slightly.

'What?'

'I'm coming over, and damn well stay put till I get there, OK? I'm sure there's nothing to worry about. He's probably just found a lady-friend who has decided that he is the love of her life...which is more than can be said for some of us,' he finished wryly. 'I won't be long.'

'There's no need...' But there was. She longed to see him. The thought of a whole night in the lonely isolation of her flat with this anxiety eating at her was dreadful.

'And if he arrives back before I get there ask him for the lady's address,' he added just before he put the phone down. 'He's obviously doing far better than me in the romance stakes.'

She literally paced the flat until he arrived, and when she opened the door to his knock and saw him leaning against the far wall, his eyebrows raised questioningly—to which she responded with a shake of her head—the impulse to fling herself into his arms in a storm of weeping was so strong that her body became rigid with control.

'Right, first things first. When did Mr Jones see him last?' Luke asked quietly as he followed her into the lounge. 'Exactly.'

'He actually saw him the evening before yesterday,' she said, as calmly as she could. 'But Mog has access to the garden himself, so he comes and goes as he wants. He could have been back some time after that.'

'And where have you looked?' he asked gently, his eyes soft as he took in the terrified golden eyes and vulnerable mouth.

'I've walked all the streets in the immediate area, calling him,' she said. 'And I checked the alley that runs at the back of the shopping precinct, and the park that's almost opposite.'

'In the dark. By yourself.' He shut his eyes for a second, and when he opened them she knew, although neither his body nor his voice betrayed it, that he was struggling not to shout at her. 'I will do everything I can to find him, Josie, but only on the condition that you don't put yourself at risk again like that. Do I have your word?' he asked flatly.

'I can't...' She stared at him as she wrung her hands helplessly before realising what she was doing and putting them quickly behind her back. 'If someone said they'd seen him—'

'You would contact me,' he said sternly. 'Wouldn't you? *Wouldn't you*? I want your promise—I mean it—or I won't lift a finger to help you.'

She stared up at him for a long moment, looking very tiny and fragile in the dim light from the standard lamp she had switched on at his knock.

She had been wandering about alleys and parks on her own? He felt murderously angry and fiercely protective at the same time, and knew he couldn't show either emotion. A tiny little thing like her would be eaten alive out there. It wasn't just down-and-outs who frequented such places, but drug addicts, perverts—and the crimes they committed when they were high on heroin and such—

He shut his mind off from the picture of her lying beneath a demented madman and repeated his warning, ice in his voice now. 'You won't act so foolishly again—promise me.' The damn cat! He'd wring its neck himself when he found it!

'I promise,' she said shakily. It felt strange to be worried over; she hadn't had anyone show any real concern for what she did for so long that she had forgotten how good it felt.

'Right. Give me the torch you used and I'll go looking for an hour or two,' he said quietly, watching her with intent, narrowed eyes and noticing the exhausted droop of her shoulders and the downward tilt to her mouth.

'I haven't got a torch,' she admitted shamefacedly, expecting a further lecture on the seriousness of her crime, but he merely stared at her for another moment without speaking, shaking his dark head slowly as though he was lost for words, before turning to leave. 'I want to come too—'

'No.' He turned in the doorway, his voice determined. 'You're all in, Josie, and I can search more quickly and thoroughly by myself.'

'I can't stay here...' she began obstinately, but when he moved back to stand in front of her, lifting her chin with a gentle finger, she fell silent.

'I can look after myself—and you, if necessary,' he said quietly. 'But I have no intention of knowingly taking you on a long and tiring jaunt at twelve o'clock at night when the dregs of London society are out and about. *I*, at least, will have a torch to light my way—I always keep one in the car—and I'll be back shortly. OK?'

'OK,' she said tremulously. 'Luke?' He paused in the act of turning away, his dark brows raised enquiringly. 'Please look as hard as you can.'

'Harder.' His lips touched hers briefly, and the spicy lemon scent of his aftershave teased her nostrils fleetingly as he left.

He returned just before three—alone—and it was all she could do to stop herself wailing out loud. 'Oh, Luke, what am I going to do?' she asked helplessly as her heart hammered painfully. 'I can't stand not knowing if he's all right. Even if he's...' She gulped but couldn't say the word. 'Even if he's hurt, I'd rather know and face it. If he's lost or—'

'What you're doing now is going to bed.' His voice was not unkind but it was implacable. 'Everything has been done that can possibly be done tonight. I've made it known in certain quarters that a reward is in the offing for a large brindle tomcat, and that might bear fruit. I'll also arrange for copies of a notice to be put in all the shops and pubs in the district to the same effect, and I'll get a couple of people knocking on doors in the area. I'll find him, Josie, I promise you.'

'But he might be...' Again she couldn't say it, her imagination running rampant as she stared at him with great tragic eyes.

'Yes, he might be,' he said gently. 'But knowing is better than not knowing, better than wondering day after day. But I don't think he's dead.'

'You don't?' she asked gratefully, aware that she would cling onto any straw, however fragile.

'No, I don't.' He touched her face with the tip of one finger. 'And you mustn't either; it won't help. Now, you're going to get some sleep and leave things to me. I'll arrange for my name and phone number to go on the notices; it'll be simpler that way.'

Simpler? She knew what he meant, what he couldn't say. If the news was bad it was better it came through to him first, so that he could prepare her for it. She stared at him as her mind sped on. Why was he being so understanding, so kind? She would be eternally grateful that he had never once said or even hinted at what he must be thinking. That Mog was only a cat, an animal.

'Thank you.' Her voice was low and shaky. 'Thank you, Luke.'

Why she moved closer to him and rested her head against the broad expanse of chest she never could explain to herself afterwards. In view of what she'd decided, about the way things *had* to be, it was insane, but in those few moments in the early morning, when the world outside was dark and distant, she forgot the past and the future. There was only the present. And she wanted him. Needed him. Loved him.

She felt him stiffen for a long moment before his hands came round her to hold her tight, but his touch was gentle as he stroked the top of her head and his voice was soft. 'It's all right. I'll make it all right. Go to sleep now and try not to worry any more.'

It was her exit line and she knew it, but she didn't take it. Instead she lifted her face up to his, her eyes luminous as she looked into his searching gaze for a moment before shutting them, the invitation blatant.

'Josie...' His voice was a low groan. 'Go to bed.'

For answer she whispered his name as she snaked her arms round his back, pressing herself further into his hard frame as she did so. There was one moment when she thought he wasn't going to respond, and then he crushed her to him and took her lips in a kiss that was almost savage, all control gone.

One night. One night wasn't too much to ask for a lifetime in which she would have to continue alone, was it? she asked herself desperately. She wanted his warmth, his comfort, his need of her this night more than any other, when her heart was rent in two at the thought that even Mog had been taken from her. She knew he didn't love her, but she loved him and that would have to do—

And then her mind stopped thinking as sensation washed it clean of everything but the touch and taste and feel of him.

His lips burnt her skin, moving over her exposed and vulnerable throat, and down into the hollow between her breasts, which were tingling at his touch. His hands urged her hips into him, the movement primitive and fierce, before moving to peel her blouse aside and then slowly caressing her fullness. 'Josie...' He breathed her name against her skin as his mouth moved to hers again, and she knew the thrilling excitement that was filling her was in him too as she sensed the heat in every nerve and sinew of his male frame.

She clung to him tightly, giving him back kiss for kiss, allowing him to penetrate the inner sweetness of her mouth while she strained against his hardness, their bodies locked close as they swayed together in the dimly lit room for endless minutes. Quite when she sensed rather than acknowledged with her mind that he had regained that iron control of his she wasn't sure, but gradually she became aware that the arms holding her against him were restraining rather than passionate, that his desire was checked and contained.

'Luke?' She raised drowning green-flecked eyes to the glittering silver of his.

'It's not enough, Josie. Your gratitude is not enough.' As she moved to jerk out of his arms they tightened, his eyes narrowing on her flushed face. 'No, there will be no misunderstanding about this,' he said levelly, his voice controlled although the fierce pounding of his heart against his ribcage was anything but. 'I want you. Make no mistake about that. I want you so badly I am thinking, eating, sleeping you twenty-four hours a day, and it's been like that since the first moment I laid eyes on you. But, like I said at the château, your body is not enough.

'You are feeling desperate tonight, anguished, and you reached out for comfort, didn't you...? Didn't you?' he persisted softly, nodding slowly as she whispered an affirmative through numb lips. 'And that is understandable. It is perfectly understandable,' he said, with a curious lack of expression she didn't like. 'And I am here for you. I will continue to be here for you.'

He took a step back, his hands still holding her arms but his body removed from her. 'But when I have you—*and I will have you*—it will be solely and utterly because you want me in the same way I want you.'

'And if I can't?' she whispered faintly, her heart breaking.

'You will.' Just for a moment that supreme arrogance showed through the calm.

'Because you always get what you want?' she asked numbly. 'Because your wealth, your power can buy anything and everyone?'

'No.' He eyed her expressionlessly. 'Because I can make whatever has gone wrong for you right. However this other man failed you, however deep the hurt is, I can deal with it. I know it.'

That utter faith in his own ability, that almost insolent arrogance, didn't grate on her as it had done before she'd acknowledged that she loved him. Now it pierced through her, causing such pain that she was unable to hide it, her eyes wounded as they held his. She would give the world if it were true, but whatever he did, whatever price he paid materially, physically, emotionally, he couldn't give her back what the surgeon's knife had taken. And if he felt anything for her—and there seemed to be tenderness and concern there, at least—what would such knowledge do to such a proud, forceful man?

'I—think you had better go, Luke.'

A deadly silence followed her broken words and then he nodded, and his voice was steady when he spoke.

'I think so too, but I will be back, OK? Again and again and again.' She hadn't expected those words and they hung in the air, tangible and threatening. 'I won't give up.' He walked across the room, turning in the doorway to survey her through eyes that were hooded and rapier-sharp. 'I never do.'

to the air, the pale and quivering. 'I won't give up the
waiting motive also hysterical, rushing in the driven to have
the attack I have that, may were resolve and there when
river on.

CHAPTER NINE

THURSDAY was a day she endured with gritted teeth, both
dreading and longing for the moment when she opened the
door that evening.

There was a mountain of work waiting for her concerning the *Night Hawk* project when she got into the office,
but the chaotic pace helped overall, although the lack of
sleep the night before had her light-headed by the time she
left the office at five sharp. And the flat was empty.
Sickeningly, stomach-wrenchingly empty.

She forced herself to make a sandwich that went straight
in the bin, swallowed a couple of aspirins for her blinding
headache, then went to lie down on the bed to rest her aching
head before she started ringing round some neighbours. She
had found that the only way she could function that day
was to blot all thoughts of Luke out of her mind, and now,
as she slipped into a deep, dreamless slumber, even her subconscious obeyed the unspoken order.

When a loud and unrelenting knocking at her front door
brought her out of thick waves of unconsciousness, it also
brought her awareness of hard, driving rain against the
window and the knowledge that the room was in darkness.
She glanced at her bedside clock as she rose groggily to her
feet and was amazed to find that it was nearly midnight,
but such was her exhaustion that it didn't even occur to her
to wonder who was banging with such ferocity so late when
she swung open the door.

'One repentant sinner.' Luke was there, big and dark,
and in his arms was a bedraggled, thin but very much alive
Mog. 'He's been badly frightened, he's hungry, and I think
he wants plenty of tender loving care, but other than that
he's fine,' Luke said calmly as he deposited the miaowing
cat in her arms. 'And don't open the door at this time of

night without enquiring who it is,' he added as he turned to walk towards the stairs.

'*Luke!*' She stood in dazed wonder as he turned, Mog clinging like a monkey around her chest and neck, his two front paws resting either side of her throat as he purred an express train of a greeting. 'How...? When—?'

'One of those notices came up trumps in a corner shop,' Luke said lazily without moving towards her, the water dripping off his black hair onto his leather jacket. 'Some kids had heard a cat miaowing from a row of garages a couple of streets away and one of them told his mother, who put two and two together after seeing the notice. She rang me this evening but we couldn't get into the place—apparently the owners have gone on holiday for a couple of weeks.

'Mog must have crept in there—probably hunting mice, because the area's crawling with vermin—when they were packing the car. They left and he was shut in. So I got the police involved and after a certain amount of persuasion a couple of the local bobbies forced an entrance and...' he indicated Mog, who was engaged in blissful contemplation of Josie's chin '...here he is.'

'I don't know what to say. How can I ever thank you?' she said shakily. 'He would have died in there, wouldn't he? Please come and have a coffee while I feed him—'

'Josie, a saint I am not,' he said wryly, a twist to his hard mouth. 'Nor am I a masochist. You might not know it, but you look good enough to eat all ruffled and dishevelled the way you are now, and self-torture is not my style. Besides, I was rather proud of my exit last night; I'm not usually so noble. So if you don't mind we'll make it some other time.'

'I— Luke... Thank you.' She wasn't making any sense but he nodded coolly.

'Goodnight, Josie.' He pointed at Mog. 'And don't forget, plenty of tender loving care. We males aren't always as tough as you think, you know.' And on that enigmatic note he left her.

*   *   *

Over the next week, when she didn't hear a word from Luke either by letter or phone, Josie went through every emotion known to man every day, every hour, on the hour—until she was emotionally and physically drained.

She had expected... She didn't know *what* she had expected, she admitted to herself the following Thursday evening, a full week after Mog's return. A pressing of his advantage? A display of that clever, ruthless strategy she had seen him display more than once? An invitation to dinner or the theatre or *something* at least...

And then, on the Friday morning, when Andy slung a newspaper on her desk with a wry comment, she thought she had the reason for his lack of interest. 'He's a wily one, is Luke Hawkton. I wonder if it's genuine?'

'What?' She glanced from Andy's round face to the picture in the paper and then froze, her heart thumping as though she had been kicked in the chest.

She recognised the girl with him, of course, the girl who was draped over his arm like a second skin as she smiled prettily into the camera, her dark hair snaking round her shoulders and her evening dress displaying more than a little of her wares. So that was who he had been with when she had been wondering if he was thinking of her. She should have known. *She should have known!* Bitterness rose up like a grey fog over the picture.

'All the "happy ever after" spiel they come out with at times like this,' Andy said impatiently. 'Hawkton is no fool. He knows the best way to shut the inquisitive mouths of the Press.'

'I don't know what you're talking about, Andy,' Josie said woodenly as she strove not to let her feelings show.

And she had begun to believe him. To believe he actually cared a bit about her. In fact she had started to worry *for* him, her love causing a biting anxiety that if he did care, *really* care, she was going to hurt him, cause him pain—

'I'm talking about Catherine Morley, of course,' Andy said irritably. 'Her engagement.'

'She's *engaged* to Luke?' Josie asked as the words registered like a bullet in her heart.

'Luke?' Andy stared at her as though he thought she was from a different planet. 'What the hell are you talking about, Josie? Why would he get engaged to his sister?'

'His sister?' If she hadn't been sitting down she knew she would have fallen down. As it was, her whole body felt peculiarly heavy, as though she was going to faint at any moment. 'Luke hasn't got a sister. He had a brother, but he hasn't got a sister.'

'I don't know what you're mumbling about.' Andy was definitely irritated now. 'I don't know about any brother, but I *do* know Catherine Morley is his sister—or his half-sister, to be exact. The papers were full of it a few months back—you must remember?'

'I don't.' She stared at Andy's fast-receding hairline as her mind spun. 'Why was it in the papers?'

'Because Catherine Morley is the love-child Luke Hawkton's father kept quiet about for years,' Andy said with heavy patience. 'For crying out loud, Josie, it was the scoop of the year for the journalist who dug it out.

'The Hawkton family insisted that the father had told them all years and years ago, when the kid was born as a result of a brief affair with some distant relation of his wife. They say the girl in question married a man she loved and Catherine was brought up as that man's child but with the knowledge of who her real father was. When she attended old Hawkton's funeral some smarty-pants on one of the tabloids started digging and it all came out. According to Luke Hawkton, Catherine is accepted as part of the family and there's no big deal.'

'Then that's the way it is, I'm sure,' Josie said carefully.

'Maybe...' Andy glanced at her before scooping the paper off her desk. 'Anyway, Catherine's just got engaged to some titled Italian guy, so she should be happy enough. Now, how's that report going?' he asked abruptly.

Once Andy had left and she was alone Josie sat staring blindly at the desk as her mind dissected the information it had been given. That day at the château, as they had chatted about his family, he had given her the reason for his father's betrayal of his mother, although she hadn't realised he was doing so at the time. And he had understood both his parents, she thought with a sudden rush of emotion that caused her chest to tighten. He hadn't judged either of them and it was clear he held no animosity for Catherine or her mother either. He had a big heart, an understanding heart.

She felt the hot prick of tears behind her eyelids and blinked them away rapidly. She couldn't pretend any longer that he was the heartless philanderer she had first imagined, although it would be easier if she could—much easier. And she had so misjudged him about Catherine...

She shut her eyes tightly. But it didn't make any difference; in fact it merely strengthened her resolution that she had to stay away from him. Everything she had learnt about him made her realise she could trust herself less and less where he was concerned. It was only distance that held any safety.

So when Luke called her, later that night, she kept her voice calm and pleasant, although her heart was pounding in her throat. 'I've been away in the States for a few days— one of the inevitable panics that occurs from time to time,' he said lazily after enquiring as to how she and Mog were. 'I wondered if you'd care to have dinner tomorrow evening?'

'Sorry, I can't.' Josie took a deep breath and spoke evenly. 'I'm going to be frantically busy over the next few weeks if everything is going to come off on the big day.'

'Not so busy you won't take time to eat, surely?' His voice was still lazy but with a tiny edge that caught at her heartstrings. 'I'll whisk you straight back home afterwards, I promise,' he added softly. 'Back to your chaste little bed— alone.'

'No, I really can't.' Mog chose that moment to come and stand by her legs, his great eyes reproachful as he stared up at her, which didn't help at all.

'OK. Goodnight, Josie.' His voice was suddenly very cold, and as the phone went down she felt a sick feeling in her chest that rose up into her throat in a stranglehold.

'It's no good you looking at me like that,' she said sharply to Mog, who had sat down with an air of censure. 'I know you like him—*I* like him, and that's why I can't see him. Surely you can see that?' Mog stared at her for a full minute

without blinking, and then turned away with an expression
of condemnation before he stood up and sauntered out of
the room, his tail very straight and disapproval expressed
in every line of his sleek body.

The next week passed, and then the next, and the only
contact she had with Luke was by telephone or in brief,
curt meetings where he was very much the remote tycoon
and kept everyone on their toes, rushing about hither and
thither.

She flew out to France twice in the next few weeks, but
made sure her schedule could be accommodated in day-
trips which didn't necessitate an overnight stay. She informed Luke's secretary each time she planned to go, but
he didn't join her as she had half expected, and wanted.
She was eating less, sleeping less, working harder—and more
confused than she had ever been in the days following the
accident.

August came, blazed brightly and left, and in the second
week of September she woke up one morning to the knowledge that it was her twenty-ninth birthday and she was more
miserable than she had been in the whole of her life. She
had refused several invitations to go out with friends, using
work pressure as an excuse, but as she sat eating her
breakfast, with Mog lying in a patch of sunlight at her feet,
she wished she had accepted one of them.

But there was only one person she wanted to be with at
the moment. And she had given him a very firm and very
definite elbow.

The postman brought a whole host of cards just before
she left for work, along with two packages from old work-
mates who had moved to distant pastures, and one from
the old aunt she corresponded with. There were more cards
and presents waiting for her at the office, and when Andy
and Mike insisted on taking her out for lunch she didn't
protest, unable to keep back a tear when they presented her
with a magnificent bouquet at the table, along with an en-
velope containing a very hefty cheque.

She had lots of good friends, she told herself that
afternoon as she sat working at her desk, her head reeling

a little from the effects of a champagne lunch; people who cared. Her career was blooming, she had no financial worries, so why did she feel as though the sky had just fallen in on her?

'Deep in work, as always. I hope it's the *Night Hawk* project you're poring over so intently?'

Her head snapped up so sharply that her neck muscles twanged as Luke's deep, husky voice sounded from the open doorway.

'Hello.' Her eyes drank in the sight of him. It had been two weeks since their last office meeting, when ten other people had been present and Luke had appeared in a foul mood.

He didn't seem to be in a foul mood today, she reflected silently as she let her eyes indulge themselves a second or two longer before dragging them away. The hard mouth was smiling slightly, the silver-grey eyes were watchful but not cold, and he wasn't in his normal immaculate suit but in casual loose trousers and a black silk shirt under the black leather jacket he had been wearing the night he had returned Mog. He looked devastating. Deliciously, overwhelmingly devastating.

'Hello.' He wandered lazily into the room, walked up to her desk and leaned over her papers, his hands either side of her on the hard wood as he kissed her very thoroughly before raising his head and standing back a pace. 'Nice, very nice,' he said appreciatively as she stared at him still in a state of shock. 'But it's your birthday, not mine...' He reached into his pocket and handed her a small giftwrapped package with a lazy smile.

'How did you know?' she asked dazedly.

'That it was your birthday?' The smile deepened, but his voice was not smiling and there was something in the deep, husky depths that made her legs weak and her lower stomach melting-soft. 'That was easy. Office records state all sorts of surface things like that.'

'Do they?' She stared at him for a moment more before she unwrapped the package with trembling fingers to reveal a small box. He'd bought her a present! Suddenly, and quite irrationally, it was the most wonderful birthday of her entire life. 'What is it?' she asked tentatively.

'Open it and see; it won't bite.' He moved to sit on a corner of the desk, and as the faint scent she had come to associate with him teased her senses—a mixture of subtle aftershave, male skin and something else that she couldn't define but which made her legs distinctly wobbly—she smiled weakly.

'Thank you...' she began as she raised the lid of the box, only to find herself speechless as she gazed down at the exquisite emerald it contained, the brilliant green jewel hanging from a fine gold chain and flashing its magnificence like wild fire.

'To bring out the colour in your eyes,' Luke said softly as he watched her cheeks turn rosy pink. 'I thought of a diamond originally, then an opal, but for the design I wanted they looked too much like teardrops, and something tells me you've had enough tears in your life without me giving you any more, so...' He took the chain from her nerveless fingers and fastened it carefully round her neck. 'An emerald it is.'

'I can't accept this.' She raised stunned eyes to his. 'It must have cost a fortune—'

'Oh, it did. I'm quite bankrupt.' He grinned at her rakishly.

'But, Luke—'

'Accept it, Josie, please.' He wasn't smiling any more, and there was something in his glance that made her toes curl. 'It would give me great pleasure to think of you wearing it sometimes. Partly because...' He raised a quizzical eyebrow as he paused, then said, 'You will have to think of me, however fleetingly, on those occasions.

'You have worked hard on the *Night Hawk* project,' he continued as she still stared worriedly at him, 'and it was very important to me to get it right—to my mother too. We both know how much it would have meant to my father. So, the necklace is just a thank-you, if you would prefer to think of it like that. A small bonus for a job well done.'

'A small bonus?' She shook her head as she allowed a wry smile to play round her lips at the easy way he had explained away such a magnificent gift. 'If it gets out how you view a "small bonus" you are going to be inundated with requests from people desperate to work for Hawkton Enterprises.'

'But they won't all have hair like red silk and golden eyes with flecks of green, will they?' he said, in such a conversational tone that the import of his words didn't strike home for a second or two. 'Do you have a coat?' he added coolly.

'A coat?' Her face was as blank as her voice.

'For the wearing of?' He eased himself off the desk and walked casually to the door. 'Because I'm taking you out to dinner...early.'

'I can't go now—'

'Oh, but you can, and you are.' He turned, and there was that quiet, calm determination in his face that wouldn't take no for an answer. 'Andy and Mike are delighted to have you leave before them for once; you make them feel most inadequate, you know.'

He spotted her coat in the corner of the room and flicked it off the hanger with his finger before slinging it across to her. 'Put it on and be quiet, there's a good girl. We'll call in and feed that striped hunter of yours on the way, of course. I've some salmon for him in the car.'

'*Salmon?*'

'I promised him some when I hauled him out of that stinking garage,' Luke said matter-of-factly. 'I figured I owed him. It's not often a man's given such a chance to impress his lady love, is it? It did impress you, I hope?' he added mockingly.

'Luke, this is crazy,' she said helplessly as she slipped her arms into her coat. 'You know there's no point—'

'Everyone can be a little crazy sometimes—didn't you know?' He smiled in satisfaction as she walked across the room towards him, the emerald glowing in the hollow of her throat like a green flame. 'And this is your birthday. This is your turn to be crazy. Besides which, according to one of my close friends, who was the only one with the nerve to tell me, I've become impossible to be around the last few weeks.' He smiled cynically with his mouth but the smile didn't reach the intent, narrowed eyes. 'So I decided I needed another fix.'

'Another fix?' She stared up at him as she reached his side, tiny and fragile against his hard bulk.

'Another fix of the drug called Josie Owens,' he said coolly. 'It's the very devil, but once you've had a taste...'

Mog viewed the salmon with something approaching ecstasy, winding ingratiatingly round Luke's legs as he tipped it onto a saucer and then making a thorough pig of himself as he ate it without pausing for breath.

'Right, that's one satisfied customer,' Luke said easily, his eyes glinting at Josie as she stood watching him in the kitchen doorway. 'Now bid him a fond farewell and we'll be off.'

'I can't go like this.' She glanced down at her office clothes in horror. 'I must change first, Luke. Is it formal or informal?'

'Informal. Definitely informal.' His eyes were warm. 'And you look fine to me.'

'No, really. I must just freshen up.' She fled to the bedroom, pulled off the neat tailored blouse and skirt she had worn all day and opened her wardrobe door as she kicked off her high heels. And then she froze as she caught sight of herself in the mirror. Was that bright-eyed, flushed, radiant girl really her? A trickle of dark warning iced down her back. She had to be careful—so, so careful. She had been right when she had called this craziness; it was. Mad, dangerous insanity.

She glanced down at herself, deliberately folding back her bikini pants and running the tip of a trembling finger along her scar. There could be no future in this, not ever—not even if Luke himself wanted it that way. He wanted children, a family, an heir one day; he had told her that himself.

And then the memory of how she had felt this morning came back in all its darkness, and she shook her head at the reflection in the mirror, her eyes suddenly hostile. There was nothing wrong with having dinner with him this once;

there *wasn't*. And she was going to. Damn it all, *she was going to*.

The rebellious mood lasted until Luke drove the Mercedes through two massive iron gates set in an eight-foot-high brick wall, having opened the fortress from the car by remote control, and proceeded along a long, curving drive which finished in front of an elegant, Georgian-style mansion surrounded by leafy trees and smooth green lawns.

'This is your house,' she said flatly as reality dawned.

'Frequented by a resident housekeeper and her handyman husband along with several cats, in case you're worried you will be all alone with the big bad wolf,' Luke drawled mockingly. 'Mrs Hodges has been in the kitchen all day preparing for tonight, so don't throw a wobbly on me now,' he added warningly.

The interior of the house was stunning, as she had known it would be, from the uniquely beautiful galleried entrance hall to the large, high-ceilinged reception rooms, right through to the massive olde-worlde kitchen, where Josie met the redoubtable Mrs Hodges, flushed and busy, in an atmosphere that was redolent with the smells of delicious home cooking. Traditional elegance was married with a softer, more homely feel, the effect of which was heightened by the presence of several plump, well-fed cats in the luxurious drawing room who were lying in cosy harmony around a roaring log fire.

She loved it all, but then she had known she would. He lived here, after all.

'It's very nice,' she said stiffly as he gestured for her to be seated in the drawing room. 'Lovely.'

'Thank you.' That quizzical look was back in his eyes as he watched her sit on the very edge of a soft cream leather sofa, her knees pressed tightly together and her hands resting primly on her lap. 'I know you don't usually drink, but as it's your birthday...' He indicated a bottle of vintage champagne resting in the cradle of its ice bucket at one side of the cocktail cabinet. 'One glass, perhaps?'

She wanted to say no—tonight more than any other she needed to stay fully alert and razor-sharp—but it would have been too rude, so she nodded smilingly, and when she sipped the faintly pink, icy-cold liquid a moment or two later it tasted like silky, sparkling nectar, in no way resembling the champagne of lunchtime. 'It's—'

'Very nice? Or lovely?' He was laughing at her, she realised suddenly, but not in the caustic, cynical way she imagined was almost habitual with him. His face was tender, gentle even, his eyes warm. And it frightened her.

She continued to feel frightened, in an excited, breathless way, through the rest of the evening. The meal was superb, served in an elegant, wood-panelled dining room amid gleaming silver cutlery, sparkling glassware and the heady scent of hothouse flowers from the bowl of expensive blooms in the middle of the table.

Luke was the perfect host—attentive, witty, setting out to entertain and amuse. And that was fine; she could cope with that. But then, as the meal progressed and they finished the first bottle of champagne and began on the second, he talked of his childhood, his parents, and then of his hopes, his dreams, and she realised the thin ice she had been skating on all evening was getting more fragile by the minute.

'How old were you when you moved away from that little village in Sussex?'

Josie's stomach clenched tightly. She had been anticipating and dreading this moment all evening, and now it was here she still didn't know how to handle it.

'College age,' she said shortly. 'Mrs Hodges really is a wonderful cook. You are very fortunate to have two housekeepers who—'

'Why do you do that?' His voice was very deep and very soft.

'Do what?' she asked carefully.

'You know what I'm getting at, Josie. The past is like a closed book with you.' He leant forward slightly, his eyes drawing hers into their hold in spite of herself. 'That was a typical answer—"college age". That could mean anything from sixteen to sixty. In fact it's no answer at all. What are you so defensive about anyway? What happened? And when?'

'Luke—'

'No, don't "Luke" me.' He took a deep breath before shaking his head slowly. 'Tell me to go to hell, get angry, shout, scream—but don't go into that impenetrable shell of yours. I know what you are really like, Josie. You can't hide from me. I won't let you. I know.'

This was too deep, too serious. She forced a bright smile and spoke lightly as she gripped her hands together tightly under the tablecloth, her nails biting into the soft flesh of her palms. 'Well, clever old you, and what do you think you know? What am I? Career woman? Frustrated housewife? Or perhaps—'

'You're the woman I want to marry.'

The words hung in the air, stark and naked, as they stared at each other across the table, and she felt her heart stop and then hammer on at a pace that made her light-headed. She couldn't speak or move; even her thought process seemed frozen. She merely stared at him with huge, stunned golden eyes, her face stricken.

'I knew it the first moment I saw you,' he continued after a long minute had ticked by in absolute silence, his mouth twisting a little at her patent horror. 'And the knowledge swept away all the principles of a lifetime. I used to be adamant that there was no such thing as love at first sight, but then it happened to me—*me*, Luke Hawkton, thirty-five-year-old cynic and man of the world. And I do love you, Josie. I love you more than—'

'Don't.' It was merely a whisper but it stopped him in his tracks when he saw the anguish in her face. 'Please don't.'

'Why?' He kept his voice cool with an effort that made his mouth white. 'You have to hear it as it is, just once. And don't say you feel nothing for me because I don't believe that; you aren't that good an actress. I've tried not to rush you, to keep my distance and give you time, but hell—' He took a deep, shuddering breath. 'I have to at least tell you how I feel, tell you that you're different.'

Oh, she was different all right. His words hit her full in the chest and he saw the impact of the blow in her eyes a second before she rose, with trembling, painful dignity, from the table.

'Luke, this is pointless,' she said shakily. 'I can't— I don't want to marry you or anyone else. I told you that. I *told* you.' The control slipped for a moment, and what he saw under the fragile exterior appalled him, but even as he reached out to her she drew back, her body rigid. 'Please take me home.'

'No.'

Her eyes shot to his face and she saw that he was shaking his head slowly, his silver eyes narrowed and intense on her face and his mouth a thin line in the hardness of his jaw. 'Luke—'

'I mean it, Josie,' he said grimly. 'You aren't leaving this place till I get some answers.'

'You've got no right—'

'Probably not, but that's never worried me before and I don't intend to let it start worrying me now.' The touch of arrogance helped, putting iron in her backbone and steadying her shaking legs. Luke the tender lover she had no defence against, but the forceful, ruthless tycoon the world knew was a different matter.

And then it came to her. The one way she could walk out of this house and his life for good. But could she do it? Could she bear him thinking—?

'I'm involved with someone else,' she said flatly, not giving herself a chance to think any more about what she was doing.

'I don't believe it.' His eyes raked her face, searching and intuitive. 'I've never seen or heard a thing to substantiate that—'

'You wouldn't have.' She could feel the blood thundering in her ears and willed herself to go through with it. 'He's married—very married. If his wife found out it would be the end of his career, his future, and then there's the children...'

'He's got children?' His voice was expressionless, strange, and she went deeper into the lie, willing her voice to sound ashamed, broken...

'Four, and all quite young. We didn't mean it to happen, for us to fall in love, but it was just one of those things—'

'One of those things?' Dark, furious colour seared the
hard cheekbones savagely and his voice was rapier-sharp.
'What the hell do you mean, "one of those things"? There
is always a point where you know, where you can draw
back...' Now his face was black with rage, his voice barely
coherent. 'And I thought you were so straight, so virtuous
compared to Charlotte Montgomery and the like. What a
laugh you must have had about that! At least she and her
kind make no secret of what they are, but you—' a bitter
disgust had turned his face grey '—you're the worst sort
of liar there is.'

'You forced me to tell you.' The pain in her heart was
physical, reaching every part of her, but she had to go
through with it. Terrible though this was, it was the only
way out. Because she couldn't tell him the truth, she
couldn't, and if he believed this he would leave her alone,
meet someone else, someone he *could* fulfil those dreams
of a family with, someone—

'I could kill you, do you know that?' He had moved
round the table to stand in front of her, and as she shrank
from the bitter contempt and anger in his face he gave a
short, hard bark of a laugh. 'But don't worry, I won't. And
do you know why? Because you aren't worth it. You aren't
worth soiling my hands on.' He stared at her for one more
moment before stalking from the room, his face fiery.

'We'll forgo coffee,' he added over his shoulder as he
reached the door. 'Arnold will take you home when you're
ready.' And then the door closed. With a softness that was
more chilling than any rage.

CHAPTER TEN

Josie existed in abject, black misery for the next few weeks, and the strain of keeping it hidden, of maintaining a bright, efficient image at work, brought her near to breaking point in the last week of October, when she was due to fly out to oversee the launch.

She hadn't seen or spoken to Luke since the night of her birthday; all their communication had been through faxes, letters and his iceberg of a secretary, although she had had the strangest feeling more than once that a pair of unseen eyes were watching her every movement. It was stupid, she knew it was stupid, but the sensation persisted right up till the day she flew out to France, alone.

She had reserved a room in a fairly mediocre hotel for the duration of her five-day stay, along with a hire car to be delivered to coincide with her arrival. The thought of staying at Luke's château was inconceivable, although his secretary had made it clear, on more than one occasion over the last few weeks, that it would be expected of her.

But no way, Josie thought grimly as the plane disgorged its passengers into the airport terminal. The next few days were going to be horrendous enough as it was. She felt the sickening lurch to her stomach that accompanied all thoughts of Luke, and took a few deep breaths, her face pale.

Before leaving the dining room that night six weeks ago she had taken off the necklace he had given her, leaving it carefully spread out on her white linen napkin where it would be seen by Mrs Hodges, along with a short note on paper she had torn out of the notebook in her handbag. 'I'm sorry.'

Such inadequate words for the hurt she had inflicted, she thought miserably, but so much better than the nightmare of watching him realise the truth, seeing the budding

knowledge in his face that he had made a terrible mistake,
that she was incapable of fulfilling his plans and aspir-
ations, that he couldn't marry her. Either that or he would
go through with his declaration, make the supreme sac-
rifice, give up the possibility of the Hawkton heir, the
children he had spoken of more than once. And either way
she wouldn't be able to bear it. Not loving him as she did.

The formalities over and her suitcase and bags collected,
she walked towards the massive glass doors, intending to
pick up her hire car and go to her hotel, when a touch on
her arm brought her head swinging round. *'Mademoiselle?'*
Louis, Luke's French chauffeur, smiled at her easily. 'I take
the bags, eh?'

'Louis?' She stared at him in surprise before glancing
hastily round her. 'What are you doing here? Are you
waiting for someone?'

'You, *mademoiselle.*' He nodded towards the doors, his
handsome face beneath the gold chauffeur's cap bland as
he wrestled the suitcase and bags from her in one easy
movement. 'The car is outside.'

'But—' She realised he was already moving away and
had to move quickly to catch him up, trotting along at his
side as she tried to get his attention. 'Louis? I'm not supposed to be met,' she protested breathlessly.

'Here we are, *mademoiselle.*' The Rolls was waiting in
what looked suspiciously like a no parking area, and Louis
had lifted the luggage into the back before she could stop
him, opening the door for her as she stood hesitating on
the pavement, her face troubled. *'Mademoiselle?'* He gestured towards the interior of the car and she glanced at him
one more time before sliding defeatedly into its luxurious
depths. But she wasn't going to the château, if that was the
plan. No way, no how.

Once they were out of the airport confines she slid the
glass panel aside and spoke to the back of Louis's trim
head. 'Do you want to know the name of my hotel?'

'No, *mademoiselle,*' he answered politely.

She tried again, her heart pounding with a mixture of panic, irritation, excitement and something else she couldn't quite pin down. 'But I'm booked into the—'

'You are staying at the château, *mademoiselle*. Is all arranged. The 'otel has been cancelled, *oui*?'

'Cancelled?' she said weakly. 'But I don't understand. Is Mr Hawkton at the château?'

'No, *mademoiselle*, not till Thursday,' the level voice replied stoically.

'Oh...' She leant back against the seat for a moment. She recognised now what that other emotion was—hope—and she berated herself for it as she bit down the fierce surge of disappointment. What was the matter with her anyway? It was best that they saw as little of each other as they could until this whole miserable episode was over; that had been the whole point of her staying at the damn hotel in the first place.

Why was she being so illogical, so stupid? Luke clearly thought it was practical for her to be on hand at the château, and she had to admit it was. That was all there was to it. And if he was prepared to endure her presence for the sake of a successful launch she owed him that at least. 'Thank you, Louis,' she said flatly as she slid the panel closed.

The next two days flew by in an orderly chaos that had Josie working from dawn to dusk and then some. She fell into bed each night almost too exhausted to wash or brush her teeth, dragging herself up each morning to stand for long minutes under a cool shower and get her brain into express mode again. But by the Thursday morning, the day before the launch, everything had come together wonderfully.

The quaint old fair was established and working perfectly, the ice rink was finished, and looking far better than even Josie had expected, and all the little extras were completed and in place. Chestnut braziers, muffin stalls, hoops and kites for the children—they were all ready and standing to attention—even row upon row of neat white ice-skating boots, all the right size for each individual guest and labelled with their names.

The caterers were coming that afternoon to set up a marquee in the grounds for refreshments during the day, and also to prepare for the more traditional buffet meal in the beautiful ballroom on the launch night.

By lunchtime, when Luke was expected, there was little more for Josie to do. She always endeavoured to leave at least half a day's leeway at this stage of a project, having learnt from bitter experience that last-minute panics often filled it to the hilt, but this time everything had fitted together like clockwork. Even the *Night Hawk*, streamlined and beautiful, was waiting patiently, moored out at sea beyond the house, and the small boats that Luke had hired to bring her in amidst a veil of coloured smoke were bobbing closer to the water's edge before they all disappeared the following morning for their glorious return later in the afternoon as dusk fell.

It was nearly all finished... Josie bit her lip as she stood on the cool, powdery sand of Luke's private beach, gazing out over a grey-blue sea. And then this chapter of her life would be closed, for ever. And she would probably never see him again, never hear his voice, see those devastating silver eyes narrow...

She hugged her middle tight and bit back a moan of pain. She had chosen this way; she had *chosen* it and there was no going back now. Not that he would want her after what she had told him. And that had to be got through too—enduring the contempt and disgust in his face whenever he glanced her way, knowing she had brought his scorn and loathing on herself by her own decision—

'Beautiful, isn't it?' She froze, unable to breathe, to move, to make any sound at all as his breath touched her neck in a whisper-soft caress. 'Timeless, untouchable... The tides come in and go out, careless of anything but their God-ordained rhythm.'

His arms slipped round her waist, drawing her back against him so that his chin was resting on the top of her head as they both gazed out across the water, and but for the support of his body she would have fallen to the ground as her legs became too weak to hold her.

'You fooled me, you know.' His voice was soft, deep, almost expressionless. 'That night at my house, you fooled me completely...for a while. Until the bruised ego and wounded pride took a step backwards and I could see clearly again.'

She still didn't speak; she didn't dare, besides which she wanted nothing more for the rest of her life than to be like this with him, and she knew it would end only too soon, and once it did—reality. The bottomless pit of reality and the rest of her life to be got through, somehow.

'And that note—"I'm sorry". I don't know another woman in this world who would have left it at that. So I started digging. I hired a few private detectives.' He felt her flinch but his grip tightened as his calm, steady voice went on. 'And they dug and they dug. It took time, but yesterday I had the full facts and they had their bonus—'

'You think money can buy everything?' She swung round in his hold as he relaxed his arms just enough for her to be able to turn and face him. 'Is that what you think? Because—'

'Not everything.' And as his eyes locked with hers she knew. He had found out. Somehow he had found out. It was there in the intense silver-grey of his black-lashed eyes and in the compassionate tone of his voice. 'No, not everything, my love,' he said softly. 'Would that it could.

'Why didn't you tell me, Josie? Why that cruel cock and bull story about a married man? That didn't make sense at first—not at first. You could easily have told me the truth when I said how I felt; you didn't have to try to make me hate you. And all the rest of it that my bloodhounds dug up—the lack of men in your life, your isolation—that didn't correspond with the way you responded in my arms—'

'Stop this—stop it!' She couldn't bear it that he knew; she couldn't bear it, she thought as she struggled wildly.

'Do you care for me, Josie, even a little?' His hands were bruising the soft flesh of her arms now, but neither of them was aware of it. 'Do you? I want the truth.'

'No, no...' She turned her head this way and that, escaping the rapier light of his eyes.

'Look at me.' He shook her, snapping her head back.
'You *will* look at me, Josie, *now*. I've been to hell and back
a million times a day these last few weeks; the least you
can do is tell me if there's any chance—'

Any chance? Her heart was thundering in her ears and
she felt something break inside, the last of her control shat-
tering as she screamed at him at the top of her voice, 'What
are you talking about? Any chance! Don't you realise what
I am? What it would mean if you married me? I'm *barren*!
Barren! Empty—no good! You'd never have your heir or
those little girls you talked about, not from me—'

'Stop it, Josie.' His face had gone grey under its tan but
she couldn't have stopped if her life had depended on it,
the pain of years flowing out in a scalding river of anguish
and grief.

'Luke, there would be no hope, no possibility of ever
having children with me,' she cried desperately. *'Don't you
understand that*? The price of having me for your wife
would be too high. You would never see your child born,
hear its first cry, hold it in your arms. Never search a tiny
face, seeking to find a little bit of me, a little bit of you.
Never be able to say "my son"—'

'I know. I know all that.' If he skirted the issue now he
would lose her for ever; he knew that. Just as he had known,
the moment she lost control, that she loved him. But he
might still lose her, and that wasn't to be borne.

'No, you don't, not really.' She was gasping now, her
body shaking in his arms, and as he lowered her to the
ground he came with her, to sit with her on the beach, facing
her with his hands cupping her face as tears streamed down
her cheeks.

'I do, Josie. I understand. I've been to the hospital. I've
even spoken with consultants, medical people—'

'Then why are you putting us both through this?' she
asked desperately, closing her eyes to block out his face.
'You want a wife who can share everything with you, and
I can't even begin to do that.'

'That's cruel, my love, cruel and untrue,' he said steadily,
knowing that what he said and did in the next few minutes

would influence whether he merely existed for the rest of his life or lived. 'And I'm going to ask you again—do you love me, even a little?'

'I—' She opened her eyes to deny it, but the storm had taken something out of her and she couldn't say the words.

'Do you?' he persisted grimly.

'It makes no difference how I feel,' she whispered brokenly. 'How could I marry you when I can't give you the desire of your heart? What sort of love is that?'

'*You* are the desire of my heart,' he said emphatically. 'Just you. I can't give you back what that accident took from you, but if it hadn't happened you might never have come into my life, and I would never have known what it is to love. I've known many women throughout my life, had many liaisons, but I have never loved one of them.'

'But you would meet someone,' she protested, her voice quieter now.

'No, I never would,' he said steadily. 'There can only be you.'

'But your heir? You want children, you know you do, and your mother—'

'Will love you as I do; I promise you that. She is not a monster, merely an Italian mamma with much of the old culture in her.'

'And you're half-Italian,' she sobbed as a fresh rush of tears blinded her. 'Oh, Luke, see it how it is. Look at it clearly.'

'I am. For the first time in my life I can see things crystal-clear. Being the man I am, I don't want second-best, so if I can't have you, if you walk away from me, I'll never have anyone.' He pulled her tight against him as he spoke, his arms crushing her against his chest.

'I mean it, Josie. We can adopt children, foster— whatever. We can do all sorts of things if we're *together*, but alone—' He pushed her slightly from him his face damp. 'I don't want to be alone any more, my love; the world isn't anything without you. The thought of you living and breathing without me, or you perhaps being in the same city as me and not knowing...' He shook his head. 'Perhaps even loving someone else...'

'I wouldn't.' Second-best. He had said anyone else would be second-best, but *she* was that. Wasn't she? 'But you might see things differently in a few years. You could have any woman you wanted, children of your own—'

'I don't want children of my *own*,' he said quietly. 'I want *our* children or none at all. And that means if we adopt, if we take on the responsibility of parenthood, we'll be in it together, whatever it holds. The children would be *ours*, yours and mine.'

'Luke—'

'Don't refuse me, Josie,' he said unsteadily as he gazed down into her eyes, which were swimming with tears. 'You are my only chance. Don't refuse me. I love you so much you have to love me back.'

'I do.' She had said it, but neither of them could believe it. 'I do love you, so much.' And then he was smothering her face in kisses, his voice husky and broken as he whispered words of love against her lips until their passion rose in time with their heartbeat.

'Luke, are you sure? Sure you've thought about what this means?'

It was too fast, it had all happened too fast, and as he drew back and looked down into her face he read the doubt and uncertainty lingering there along with the desire. 'I'm sure,' he said softly. 'I actually felt relief when I found out what was really wrong, that it wasn't another man. Can you believe that? It's a terrible thing to admit when what happened affected you so badly, but the thought of another man holding you, kissing you was unthinkable. Your past is your past, and dead and gone, but a lover here in the present—'

'There has never been a lover—not ever.' And then she told him all of it—about Peter, the aftermath of the accident, the decisions she had made. And he listened without speaking and watched her face, his own tender and compassionate and rent with grief for her.

'I would have liked to kill this man.' The silver eyes narrowed as he spoke. 'In my mother's country a man who treated an innocent young girl that way would have walked from the court knowing he had to look over his shoulder until the day she was avenged. It is good he is dead.'

'It doesn't matter any more.' And it didn't. For the first time she could say it and mean it. 'He can't hurt me now.'

'No one will hurt you any more.' He gathered her to him and kissed her gently on the mouth. 'You believe me, trust me on this? You are everything I have ever hoped for in a woman, my love—*everything*,' he emphasised as she lowered her eyes and shook her head. 'This baby thing has warped the way you see yourself, how you value what you are. The gift you are giving me—of yourself—is enough for me. I know it but I have to make you know it too, and if it takes the rest of my life I will do it. And we will have children— as many as you want. We will fill our houses with them, our gardens—'

'Dogs too?' She was laughing now through her tears as for the first time she dared to allow herself to believe.

'One for each child.' He touched her face with his hand, his expression suddenly serious. 'And each child will be loved and cherished for what it is—a special gift for us. The biological part means nothing, Josie, not really. You only have to look at all the misery in natural families to see that. What counts is the bit between being born and dying. The giving, the sharing, the joys and sorrows, and most of all the love.

'When I thought I wasn't going to be able to get through to you, that you were never going to let me in, and later, when you told me there was someone else—' He stopped abruptly and breathed hard, the pain in his eyes visible and fierce. 'That was the most terrifying time of my life. I thought I'd go mad, insane. I can't manage without you. I can't hold it all together if you aren't there by my side. You have to believe that, *really* believe it.

'No one else matters but you. It is us at the beginning and it will be us at the end, and if in the time between our family brings us pleasure then that's wonderful, but that is all it is. It isn't life-sustaining. You are. Do you believe me?'

'I'm trying.' She smiled, but the tears had started again.

'You *will* believe it.' He pulled her into him as his mouth sought hers, his need fierce and raw. 'I will make you. I don't care how long it takes—I will make you. You are my perfect love, my perfect, perfect love...'

EPILOGUE

'LUKE, what if—?

'No "what ifs".' He moved swiftly across the room and took her in his arms, his face tender. 'It will be all right; trust me.'

'I'm frightened.' She looked up at him, her fist pressed against her mouth.

'You have every right to be frightened,' he said calmly. 'We're waiting to give birth and I'm petrified, but there are no hard and fast guarantees, my love—not in a biological birth and not in this one. Things can go wrong—that's life— but I'm here for you and you're here for me. Everything else takes second place. OK?'

She nodded limply as she relaxed against him, her body tiny against his bulk. 'I love you.'

'I know.' There was immense satisfaction in the deep male voice. 'I love you too.'

And as she raised her head for his mouth she felt as she always felt in his arms—loved, secure and, yes, perfect. She was enough for him. It constantly amazed her, but over the last two years since they had been married she had come to accept it as reality. His love was strong and real and its burning passion had consumed the doubts and fears that had haunted her in the early days of their marriage. Nothing could separate them, they were two halves of one mould, and in the shadowed intimacy of their big bed he had restored her faith in herself as a beautiful, desirable woman, complete and perfect in the eyes of the man she loved.

And then the telephone rang and she froze against him for one moment before he lifted his mouth from hers, his face tender and calm as his eyes searched hers. 'OK, Mrs Hawkton?' he asked softly. 'Just remember, whatever is said, I love you.'

She could read nothing from his face while he listened to the voice at the other end before murmuring a quiet, 'Thank you,' as he replaced the receiver.

'Luke?'

'They're ours.' He was across the room in two strides, picking her up in his arms and swinging her round and round until the room was a kaleidoscope of colour. 'That's it, Josie, they're ours. It's signed and sealed and official.'

And later, after they had loved and loved some more, they crept upstairs in the soft warmth of the mellow summer evening to check on their children—a little girl of three and a little boy of one, who had come to them some months before, bruised and traumatised from the accident that had robbed them of their parents and older sister.

And there were others through the years: a damaged little scrap of humanity who was all eyes and teeth and had endured more cruelty and horror in his short four-year life than most adults ever had to face; twin girls of two, whose single-parent mother had wanted to start a new life in a different country with a man who didn't want a ready-made family; a small baby girl who had been born with a facial deformity that would need countless operations before it was corrected and who had been rejected by her natural parents.

They all came and they were all loved, and, like tiny precious flowers in rich good soil, they blossomed and grew, and in their turn loved back. Because love was priceless.

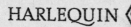

The Gentleman & The Hell Raiser

Don't miss these captivating stories
from two acclaimed authors
of historical romance.

THE GENTLEMAN by Kristin James
THE HELL RAISER by Dorothy Glenn

Two brothers on a collision course
with destiny and love.

Find out how the dust settles October 1997
wherever Harlequin and Silhouette
books are sold.

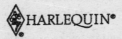

HARLEQUIN®   Silhouette®

HREQ1097

**Don't miss these Harlequin favorites
by some of our bestselling authors! Act now and
receive a discount by ordering two or more titles!**

HT#25720	A NIGHT TO REMEMBER	$3.50 U.S. ☐
	by Gina Wilkins	$3.99 CAN.
HT#25722	CHANGE OF HEART	$3.50 U.S. ☐
	by Janice Kaiser	$3.99 CAN.
HP#11797	A WOMAN OF PASSION	$3.50 U.S. ☐
	by Anne Mather	$3.99 CAN.
HP#11863	ONE-MAN WOMAN	$3.50 U.S. ☐
	by Carole Mortimer	$3.99 CAN.
HR#03356	BACHELOR'S FAMILY	$2.99 U.S. ☐
	by Jessica Steele	$3.50 U.S.
HR#03441	RUNAWAY HONEYMOON	$3.25 U.S. ☐
	by Ruth Jean Dale	$3.75 CAN.
HS#70715	BAREFOOT IN THE GRASS	$3.99 U.S. ☐
	by Judith Arnold	$4.50 CAN.
HS#70729	ANOTHER MAN'S CHILD	$3.99 U.S. ☐
	by Tara Taylor Quinn	$4.50 CAN.
HI#22361	LUCKY DEVIL	$3.75 U.S. ☐
	by Patricia Rosemoor	$4.25 CAN.
HI#22379	PASSION IN THE FIRST DEGREE	$3.75 U.S. ☐
	by Carla Cassidy	$4.25 CAN.
HAR#16638	LIKE FATHER, LIKE SON	$3.75 U.S. ☐
	by Mollie Molay	$4.25 CAN.
HAR#16663	ADAM'S KISS	$3.75 U.S. ☐
	by Mindy Neff	$4.25 CAN.
HH#28937	GABRIEL'S LADY	$4.99 U.S. ☐
	by Ana Seymour	$5.99 CAN.
HH#28941	GIFT OF THE HEART	$4.99 U.S. ☐
	by Miranda Jarrett	$5.99 CAN.

(limited quantities available on certain titles)

TOTAL AMOUNT	$ _____
DEDUCT: 10% DISCOUNT FOR 2+ BOOKS	$ _____
POSTAGE & HANDLING	$ _____
($1.00 for one book, 50¢ for each additional)	
APPLICABLE TAXES*	$ _____
TOTAL PAYABLE	$ _____
(check or money order—please do not send cash)	

To order, complete this form and send it, along with a check or money order for the total above, payable to Harlequin Books, to: **In the U.S.:** 3010 Walden Avenue, P.O. Box 9047, Buffalo, NY 14269-9047; **In Canada:** P.O. Box 613, Fort Erie, Ontario, L2A 5X3.

Name: _____

Address: _____ City: _____

State/Prov.: _____ Zip/Postal Code: _____

*New York residents remit applicable sales taxes.
Canadian residents remit applicable GST and provincial taxes.

Look us up on-line at: http://www.romance.net   HBKOD97